11/28/2020
Linda –
Congratulations!
I look forward to seeing you
back next year for book 2,
"The Children of Autumn".
Enjoy!
Claudine Marcin

The Glory Box

PINEAPPLE IN WINTER

CLAUDINE MARCIN

authorHOUSE®

AuthorHouse™
1663 Liberty Drive
Bloomington, IN 47403
www.authorhouse.com
Phone: 1 (800) 839-8640

Published by AuthorHouse 05/22/2020

ISBN: 978-1-7283-6221-2 (sc)
ISBN: 978-1-7283-6220-5 (hc)
ISBN: 978-1-7283-6219-9 (e)

Library of Congress Control Number: 2020909164

Print information available on the last page.

This book is printed on acid-free paper.

Mom,

With your enthusiasm and encouragement, I finished my first book. You are my toughest critic, my collaborator, and I respect your opinion. I appreciate you more than you know and want to dedicate this book to you, my best friend. I love you and couldn't have done it without your support.

Thank you, Mom!

Winter

The blue wind blows
in a whirlwind of chilling cold
across the pure-white plains
and the dead silence
that can be only …
winter.

Prologue

The room was dark except for the soft glow of the floor lamp enveloping Alice's body, providing just enough light for covert reading. The beautiful, leather-bound book that stood out from all other books on the bookcase was too irresistible to leave behind. She had plucked it from the shelf and snuck it back to her quarters like any experienced pickpocket.

It was cold, so Alice had wrapped herself in a wool blanket before settling in with her treasure and a large glass of red wine. The last several years had not been kind to her. The Cradle was meant to be their salvation during the Long Winter, but after so many years in isolation, it felt more like a tomb. The fire in her once blazingly vibrant ginger locks had been tamped down, and her emerald eyes had lost their luster.

The Long Winter had lasted longer than the initial estimate of five years. Alice had lost weight, having to stretch her rations, existing mostly on one small meal a day. She hungered to feel the sun's rays on her dull, ashy skin; to feel the dewy grass under her feet; to feel a warm breeze blow through her coarse hair.

She had been reading for hours, so captivated by the words and emotions on the pages. The thoughts and ideas maturing as each page told familiar stories from another's eyes. Some would see reading another's private journal as an invasion of privacy, but she was bored and didn't see much harm at this point. Besides, she desperately needed a distraction.

She pulled the blanket tighter, snuggling deeper into the plush leather of the high-backed chair as she continued reading. Shared memories of college danced across the pages and through her mind. She was reliving her own experiences; stories she had forgotten now filled her with joy. She read on about the five-day summit that reunited her with her college friend, a distant memory now.

The writer went into detail about the collaboration with Alice after the summit and how exhilarating it was; Alice thought so too. The journal was dredging up old, painful memories as well. She began to think about the accident a few years before the Long Winter began, but she quickly pushed those thoughts away, back into the darkness.

As she continued reading, she began to yawn and blinked her eyes hard in an attempt to stay awake, and then Alice turned to the next page.

The handwriting was different. The page was completely blank, except for four words scrawled in the middle. It looked like the scribbling of someone who was terrified. What did it mean? Her brow furrowed as she stared at the four words:

What have I done?

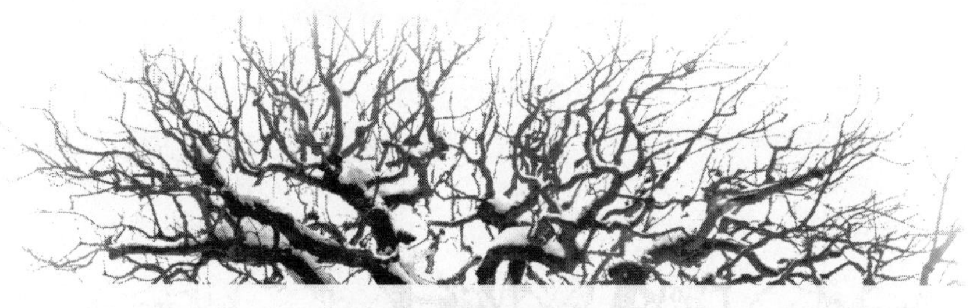

Chapter 1

Hanita watched with trepidation as one by one, the other members of the Confederation filed into the auditorium. Bobbing her foot up and down impatiently, she scrutinized them the way she regarded suspects.

They had gathered to attend a weeklong special summit concerning the future, and today was the first day. Hanita was a regional head of safety and security, but as part of the newly elected class of representatives, she had no idea what to expect.

There were no heads of state or ambassadors in attendance. There were no presidents or monarchs. The world was no longer controlled by politicians and diplomats. What remained of civilization was no longer interested in political gain or world domination. Those who remained were only interested in survival, including Hanita. This was the only world she knew.

Her auburn hair was pinned up as usual, and her long bangs, parted off center, were swept across her right cheek. Hanita leaned back in her chair, legs crossed, occupying both arms of the seat since Alice was busy scribbling in her notebook.

Alice and Hanita were good friends, representing different interests at the summit. They had arrived about thirty minutes early and selected seats in the fifth row up from the floor. They had a great view.

Alice, a doctor of biotechnology and neuroscience, wasn't interested in who was arriving. Her long, ginger hair was swept over her left shoulder, revealing the large wire-frame glasses sliding down the bridge of her nose. Since this was her third year serving on the Confederation, she pretty much knew all of the representatives.

Hanita listened as the murmurings grew louder while the seats filled in around them. She quickly tucked the loose hair behind her ear as she looked over at Alice, seated on her left. As usual, Alice was too absorbed in her own mind to people-watch, but Hanita was desperate to talk.

Humanity is now governed by a semi-direct democracy where the people decide on policy while the Confederation administers day-to-day governance. Created about eight decades ago, the Confederation was really still in its infancy.

Originally consisting of one hundred members of various officers of the law, it's now up to three hundred representatives from the fields of science, technology, and medicine as well as law enforcement. Members include theorists, philosophers, climatologists, and engineers, all highly respected in their fields. Each member of the Confederation is nominated and elected by their peers to represent their specialized field and make decisions for the benefit of humanity.

Some did not want to serve, but Hanita was proud to. And no one campaigns for the job; however, once elected, you serve a four-year term on the Confederation. Although nominated representatives are not voted on by the people, the citizens do hold recall power over any representative they feel is unfit to serve on the Confederation.

The obligation to serve comes with its burdens. Members are sometimes required to step away from research and development, patients and surgery. This is what led to the Confederation imposing four-year term limits. Term limits ensures new and fresh ideas continue to be represented, but more importantly, it allows members to return to the full-time work they had set aside. If necessary, terms may be extended in order to complete debates and votes on discussions that began prior to the end of a member's term.

It was unusual for the entire Confederation to come together like this outside of the normal scheduled quarterly sessions. They usually held small symposiums or videoconference with each other when a new, urgent matter needed to be discussed. This special summit was different and required all representatives to be in attendance.

Several presentations and meetings were planned during the week with various speakers. In the end, the Confederation anticipated they would draft a compulsory referendum resulting in a binding vote, but about what? That remained a mystery.

The briefing today was arranged by Dr. V. Boyd and was scheduled to begin at fourteen hundred hours. The auditorium was configured to accommodate 330 people in ten rows of thirty high-backed folding seats positioned in front of a stage. The lights were up as invitees were still arriving: Department heads, deputies, assistants, secretaries. It looked like the auditorium would be filled to capacity.

"Who is this Dr. Boyd, anyway?" Hanita wondered out loud while looking around impatiently. He hadn't arrived yet and the presentation was scheduled to start in five minutes.

"Huh?" Alice grunted, as she kept writing.

"Dr. Boyd," Hanita repeated, nudging Alice with her elbow. "He's probably some stuffy old bookish type," she speculated, glancing down at the notepad on Alice's lap.

Alice stopped writing and flopped back in her seat as she looked comically at Hanita. She caught sight of a tall figure entering the stage from their right. "I believe that's him," she said, pointing with her pen.

Hanita turned her attention down front to the man striding across the stage. He walked with purpose, as if the stage belonged to him. He was wearing a blue button-down shirt, sleeves rolled to mid-forearm, tucked into faded blue jeans. His left gate was slightly more pronounced than the right, likely because he was carrying a large satchel under his right arm.

Taking in the crowd in front of him, he brushed his sandy-blond bangs back from his eyes. When he reached the podium, he set the satchel down on the stage and then removed a metal thermos and a thick portfolio. He opened the thermos, took a sip from the thermos, and then placed it on the podium; he then laid down the portfolio and unfolded it in front of him.

Hanita silently studied his features, held captive by his presence. She observed fresh stubble covering his upper lip and square jaw up to his high, rounded cheekbones. He had a strong pronounced brow over deep-set eyes, cut symmetrically by a long thin nasal bridge.

Alice watched with amusement as Hanita absorbed every detail of Dr. Boyd, no longer interested in her notepad. She was used to seeing strong reactions from other women when Dr. Boyd entered a room. He was never what was expected.

"How did you say you know him?" Hanita probed, her eyes remaining on their target, watching as his long fingers fixed the tiny wireless microphone to the collar of his shirt.

"Actually, I didn't," Alice snickered as she tucked her pen into the breast pocket of the white lab coat she was wearing. "But if you must know, he's my brother."

"Brother?" Hanita snapped her head toward Alice, who was still looking at her, nodding. "You never told me you had a brother."

"I guess it just never came up," Alice replied, shrugging and folding her arms across her chest.

"But your last name isn't Boyd," she questioned, turning her attention back to the stage in time to catch Dr. Boyd look at the clock on the wall to check the time.

"Vytas uses our mother's surname," she explained.

"Vytas," Hanita repeated softly. Then she looked back at her friend and winked. "Introduce me after the conference."

Alice sheepishly agreed with a heavy sigh. She was used to that reaction as well.

Suddenly, there was a hum and squeak from the stage. They both looked down front to see Vytas adjusting the position of the microphone he was wearing while tapping on it.

"Good afternoon, everyone," he declared. His buttery voice slowly melted over Hanita, instantly relaxing her. She took a deep breath and waited for his next words.

"My name is Dr. Vytas Boyd," he continued. "Some of you know me," he went on, gazing around the room and pausing to nod at those he recognized. "For those who don't, I am a doctor of engineering and head of research in the astrophysics department.

"While I admit I do on occasion have my head in the stars," he added, laughing, "my major area of study has been physics and electrical engineering." He gestured quite naturally while he spoke, instantly creating a rapport with his audience.

"I want to welcome you all to day one of our summit." He nodded toward the audience, and they responded in a loud applause as they glanced around the room at their fellow Confederation members.

"I know many of you traveled a long way to be here," he went on while the ovation died down. "As I look around the room, I'm honored to see many respected leaders in science and medicine, as well as my colleagues in engineering and physics."

He watched as many of the Confederation members were also looking around at the other attendees, acknowledging people they recognized. "I also see there are many people here I don't know, but I hope to meet during the week."

He motioned to someone in the back of the room and asked, "Shall we begin?"

The lights dimmed in the auditorium as a large white screen rolled down from the ceiling behind him with a loud whirring noise. A single stream of light appeared from the projector in the back of the theater. Vytas squinted as the light shown in his eyes. Specks of dust were visible in the beam, until suddenly an image appeared on the screen. It was Jupiter.

"I hope you will all indulge me in a history lesson," Vytas began. The room was silent, focused on the presentation about to unfold in front of them. Their host projected charisma and confidence that commanded attention and inspired trust.

"One hundred years ago, Jupiter exploded." He paused a moment to click a button on the controller in his hand, changing the image on the screen. "At the time of the explosion," he continued, "our planets were at their closest distance, approximately 588 million kilometers apart."

With a click, the image changed again to illustrate this point.

"The explosion lasted about twelve hours," Vytas continued. "Light travels at a constant speed of 186,000 miles per second." He paused for effect while the audience pondered this fact before continuing on.

"The Western Hemisphere was fortunate in that it was facing away from the blast when it reached our planet, approximately thirty-three hours later. It was nighttime, but burning three hundred times as bright as the sun, the explosion lit up the night sky."

A new slide appeared with a blink. It compared the burning planet and the sun so the group could visualize the vast difference in brightness.

"The Eastern Hemisphere wasn't so lucky." Vytas' voice became soft as he projected empathy regarding this sensitive topic. "The effects in the

Eastern Hemisphere were immediate and catastrophic, as they experienced the full effect of the blast, with no time to prepare."

Images of the aftermath flickered on the screen. Vytas did not speak but instead observed the reactions from the audience, leaning one forearm on the podium. There were gasps as the slides revealed collapsed structures, burned homes, scorched land masses. Some attendees looked away at the sight of mass graves and people suffering from second- and third-degree burns.

"My apologies," he said sympathetically. "I know this is hard to see, but I believe it's important for us to remember." The slides continued flickering on the screen.

He steadied his voice and went on. "Communication satellites were obliterated in the blast as the light and gamma rays reached our atmosphere." More slides clicked by on the screen.

"The shock wave created by the blast, an electromagnetic pulse or EMP, didn't arrive for several weeks." He glanced backward at the screen as the images flipped by.

"The interference from the EMP disrupted electronic equipment and utilities around the world." He studied the audience reaction to the slides and then looked back at the images before continuing.

"Those who survived the initial event attempted mass deportations; however, the EMP damaged infrastructure, buildings, and transportation, which impeded our efforts to rescue survivors." Vytas hesitated while several images of the destruction flipped by on the screen. "The survivors were essentially on their own.

"High levels of radiation were detected, and survivors became sick," he paused. "Eventually, people started dying from radiation poisoning." Gruesome images of hordes of afflicted people and mass graves flashed by on the screen.

The audience stirred in their seats, making muffled comments to each other, horrified by the images.

Vytas motioned to someone in the back of the room, and with that, the beam of light went dark. The room was pitch-dark for a split-second as the lights were slowly turned up. The white screen rolled back into the ceiling with a "whir, whir, whir," and the room was again illuminated by the overhead lights.

Vytas straightened and faced the audience as he flipped the page in the portfolio in front of him and waited for his colleagues to compose themselves. After a few moments, they focused their attention back to Dr. Vytas Boyd.

"The population of our planet was over *seven billion* at the time of the explosion," Vytas emphasized with his voice and with his hand gestures. "It still isn't clear how many people died in the initial blast, but we estimate the loss of approximately four billion souls as a direct result of the explosion, including the resulting EMP."

The audience members gasped at this statistic. Vytas stepped out from behind the podium.

"Over the next several decades, land masses changed." He slowly walked toward the front of the stage. "Borders between countries were eroded away, as what remained of the population began to regroup in the Western Hemisphere.

"Millions more lives were lost around the world due to shortages of food, lack of clean water and medicine, and inadequate shelter as we continued to rebuild and recover." He looked down as he slowly shuffled to the front of the podium. He was making a connection with the audience by moving closer to them. "That's roughly 60 percent of the world's population lost due to a single event.

"None of us here today were alive to experience the devastation," he addressed the room. Looking down into the front row, he teased, "Except maybe for Dr. Wheeler," pointing at his aging mentor. The welcomed levity helped to ease the discomfort of what they had just witnessed.

"Jupiter played an important role for our planet and for the rest of the solar system," Vytas stated. "As the largest planet in our solar system, it created periodic gravitational pulls that affected planetary orbits, our planets' axial tilt and rotation, even affecting trajectories of asteroids.

"We've noticed that without Jupiter's pull, several things are happening." He turned to the side and began to slowly stride across the stage. "This is where it gets complicated." He stopped and faced the audience. "So I just mentioned rotation, tilt, and orbit; what is the impact, you ask?

"Our rotation has been gradually slowing, making the days seem longer. We've all noticed this." He nodded and gestured to the room, watching as several people acknowledged the fact. "The effect has been building up over time since Jupiter exploded, and it's happening faster than ever before.

"Additionally, with each orbit around the Sun, Jupiter swept up bits of rock and space dust that otherwise could have impacted our planet. This debris remained in Jupiter's orbit like planetary rings.

"When Jupiter exploded, all of this debris, including bits of Jupiter, was released into space." He held his hands together in front of his body, in the shape of an orb, and then he pulled them apart to simulate this fact.

"So we have two alarming facts that we have to face," he announced, holding up two fingers. "Number one, our rotation is slowing, and number two, a giant cloud of space dust is moving toward us." He held his arms outstretched to his sides.

"A hundred years ago, a single rotation of our planet took only twenty-four hours," he reminded the audience. "By our calculations, the planetary rotation will reach its peak deceleration in ten years." He paused before continuing. "At its peak, it will take 5,832 hours to make one full rotation, or what used to be 243 days."

The audience reacted with gasps and murmurs, squirming uncomfortably in their seats.

"This brings us to axial tilt." He looked around the room as he asked, "What is axial tilt, you're wondering? So we all understand there is a North and South pole.

"Axial tilt is the angle between a planet's rotational axis at its North Pole and a line perpendicular to the orbital plane of the planet." He held one arm out in front of him and bent his elbow up, tilting his arm back and forth, while he outstretched his other arm and made a fist. "Simply put, axial tilt is what causes the change of seasons, like summer and winter.

"Normally, our planet is tilted at an angle of 23.5 degrees," he stated as he tilted his arm to approximate the angle with his fist. He raised his fist and explained with a grin, "This is the sun, by the way." Muffled laughter occupied the room while he put his fist back in the right position.

"Our axial tilt has been wobbling since the initial event." He bobbed his bent arm up and down.

"Without Jupiter's gravitational pulls, two things will happen," he continued. "Our axial tilt will continue to wobble until it ends up at about

3 degrees." He raised his bent arm until it was nearly straight, directly facing his fist.

"At the same time, our orbit will drift farther from the Sun than ever before." He began pulling his bent arm farther away from his fist, creating a dramatic image of what was to come. "These two things will coincide with our longest day ever, which brings us back to the issue of rotation.

"The combination of these events will send our planet into a virtual ice age." Vytas returned to the podium and turned the pages in the folder laid out in front of him. "And it gets worse.

"Let's not forget about Jupiter's sixty-seven moons," he reminded the audience. "The four largest were sent scattering in the wake of the explosion." He moved to the other side of the stage. "The other smaller moons may have been obliterated into space dust or asteroids; we just can't know for sure. So what does all this mean for humanity?

"As the cloud of space dust passes by, we will be blanketed in a layer of carbon dioxide and sulfuric acid; we believe this will land mostly on the already uninhabitable Eastern Hemisphere.

"This brings us to Jupiter's four large moons." He raised his right hand and pointed with his index finger. "The one bit of good news is that the Galilean moons have been pulled into orbit around the Sun, like four new planets.

"Why is this good news, you ask?" He inquired, looking around the audience. "We believe that once the cloud of space dust passes us, it will actually collect around the Galilean moons. This event will essentially push our planet closer to the Sun, simultaneously correcting our axial tilt and orbit.

"The momentum of this push should also increase the planet's rate of rotation, though we don't believe we will ever again reach twenty-four hours for a single day; maybe thirty to thirty-five hours," he said, squinting his eyes and wobbling his outstretched hand.

"We estimate that it will take six to twelve months for the planet to freeze, creating the ice age I referred to earlier. It will take another three and a half to four years for the Galilean moons to push our planet, correcting the orbit and axial tilt. We are calling this four- to five-year time frame the Long Winter."

He folded his arms onto the podium and leaned onto it. "So," he continued, "how do we survive the Long Winter?"

The handsome, charismatic speaker paused a moment as he let his eyes move around the room. Then he stood tall and said, "That is why you are all here this week.

"Over the next several days, we will collaborate to solve this problem." He walked around the side of the podium and gestured over toward the exit. "As you exit the auditorium today, please pick up a copy of the material we have prepared for you.

"Read it and consider all of the facts," he said. "When we reconvene tomorrow, the real work begins."

He glanced around the room and folded his hands in front of his body, considering if there was anything more to add. "This concludes our kickoff presentation.

"We will meet back in this room tomorrow at ten hundred hours. Have a good evening, everyone," he closed, waving slightly before switching off the microphone and removing it from his shirt collar.

****

Vytas shuffled his papers together and shoved them back into the worn leather portfolio. He glanced up into the auditorium a few times, watching people stand and stretch before lumbering in between the rows of seats and down the stairs. Other attendees milled around in front of the stage, making small talk with each other before exiting through the doors on either side of the room. Some of them looked up and thanked him for the presentation.

Alice emerged from the shadowy fifth row; he noticed her familiar face and smiled. He stepped out from behind the podium and jumped off the stage onto the floor.

"Alice," he said, opening his arms, and welcomed his sister in a tight embrace. She stood on her tiptoes and kissed his cheek emphatically as she squeezed him back. He unexpectedly lifted her off the floor as he thought about how long it had been since they had seen each other.

Once her feet were firmly on the floor again, she stepped backward and motioned for Hanita to come forward. "Vytas," she announced, "this is my friend, Hanita."

He instantly noticed the black uniform she was wearing and something else: her eyes. Mysterious and dark, her eyes were tempting bites of feisty bittersweet that felt like home.

"It's a pleasure to meet you," Vytas crooned as he leaned in toward Hanita, extending his hand gently. There was no shortage of magnetism dripping from his six foot frame, but at the same time, he had a gentle touch.

Hanita shook his hand and replied, "It's good to meet you too." Glancing slyly at Alice, she offered, "I didn't know Alice had a brother."

"And I wasn't aware that Alice had such a charming friend," he said, winking at his sister. "You're in security?" he inquired, glancing at her dark jacket.

Hanita looked down, following his eyes, as she remembered she was wearing her uniform today. "Yes." Her crooked grin was warm and framed by dimples.

Hope swelled in Vytas's chest for the first time in a long time. "I would love to hear more about what you do."

Hanita murmured, "I'm sure you would find it quite mundane," as she gestured toward the stage, recalling his very detailed oration.

"My dear," Vytas declared, "you are a bright light cast upon this dark day."

Hanita's exotic olive skin, punctuated by rosy cheeks and ripe lips, had immediately beguiled the astrophysicist.

They were locked in a seductive trance. All words had escaped Hanita as she held his gaze, swooning. His words were still floating over and around them, forming a bubble that blocked out the rest of the world.

"Hanita," he recited, smiling sexily at her, still holding her hand in his. "That's a beautiful name."

"Thank you," she replied, blushing shyly. "It's a family name. It means 'Grace of the Gods,'" she continued nervously.

Alice's eyes were bouncing left and right, watching the flirtatious tennis match unfolding in front of her. They barely noticed as she announced, "I'm gonna go." She paused before stepping backward and walking off to the left, chuckling to herself.

"Have a coffee with me," Vytas proposed. "And we can discuss the ins-and-outs of your mundane career in security and our future."

"Ha," she said, laughing. "That's presumptuous of you."

"You're presuming I meant *our* future," he said, crinkling his brow and pointing at her then back at himself. "How do you know I didn't mean our, as in all of us?"

Hanita realized her hand was still wrapped inside of his. Her thumb was gently stroking his skin as she thought about how clever he was.

"So are you interested?"

Hanita nodded slowly, still smiling. "Very."

"Just one second." Vytas's hand slipped from hers as he stepped toward the stage and used his strong arms to easily pull himself up onto the three-foot-high platform. He walked behind the podium and smiled sweetly at Hanita as he collected his portfolio and stuffed it back into his satchel. He returned to the edge of the stage and hopped down onto the floor once again to join her.

"Ready?" he asked as he approached Hanita.

She nodded, and as they exited the auditorium to the left, Vytas gently placed his hand on the small of Hanita's back.

****

Alice saw Kyle Weber walking ahead of her as she exited the auditorium. He was part of the new class of representatives. She had missed the opportunity to catch up with him at the last quarterly session, and so she was looking forward to seeing him again at the summit. They hadn't seen each other since university.

"Kyle," she called out, walking faster.

Kyle turned to see Alice coming toward him, her ginger locks bouncing as she stepped. He smiled wide and stepped toward her with his arms spread open to great her. "Alice!"

They embraced tightly in the hallway as people walked by. Her cheek brushed against his bearded jawline as she inhaled the musky aroma of his skin.

Alice stepped back, her hands still around his shoulders. He looked taller now, and his curly black hair had grown longer since … *How long has it been?* she wondered. Just then, she noticed the feel of his solid shoulders. Beginning to blush, she released him and took another step backward.

“It’s so good to see you,” she blurted out, while pushing her glasses up higher on the bridge of her nose, a nervous habit.

“It’s good to see you too, Alice.” He nervously fumbled with the folder under his arm. “I didn’t expect to see you here,” he lied. He knew Alice would be here and had noticed her in the auditorium. He wanted to approach her, but all the feelings of anxiety he had while they attended university together came rushing back.

“I was hoping …” She paused to rethink her choice of words. “Would you want to have dinner together?”

Kyle was caught off-guard by the invitation. He wanted to blurt out, “Hell yes,” but the words wouldn’t come out of his mouth.

“Just to catch up,” she added, beginning to feel awkward during the long pause before his response.

“Yes,” he finally answered. “That sounds great.”

“Okay,” she sighed, smiling. “Eight o’clock?”

“Oh, I can’t do it tonight, though. I want to read over the material to prepare for tomorrow.”

Alice nodded, feeling disappointed at first, but then she remembered how Kyle was. Vytas had asked the Confederation to read the handout, so that’s exactly what Kyle would do. “Another time, then,” she agreed. “We have all week, right?”

“Definitely,” he responded. “Who’s that with Vytas?” he asked, nodding toward the exit.

Alice turned just in time to see Vytas and Hanita exit the building. Seeing them together, she wondered why she had never thought of introducing them before. Her own romantic life had always taken a back seat to her work. That’s likely the reason why she never gave much thought to it, but now, it seemed so obvious. The chemistry between them as they met was extraordinary.

Chapter 2

Vytas and Hanita settled into a small, quiet booth in the rear of the coffee shop. It was a half-moon-shaped bench, perfect for intimate conversation.

He sat sideways, pressing his left side into the red cushion and resting his left arm on the seat back. He twirled his mug of coffee in front of him as he listened to Hanita talk in between sips of chamomile tea. The relaxing aroma drowned out the rush-hour bustle in the busy coffee house.

"So where did you grow up?" he asked.

"In the south," she answered as she nervously sipped her tea. She turned her body toward him, welcoming him into her space. She pulled her legs up onto the bench, knees bent, resting her weight on her right hip as she replaced the teacup on the table and reclined into the bench.

"Tell me about your family."

"There's not much to tell," she sighed. "My parents were high-ranking security officers, and they wanted the same for me. So they groomed me from a young age to follow in their footsteps."

"So you were an only child," he deduced.

"Yes," she replied, sounding a bit disappointed for not having a sibling. "My parents couldn't have other children after me." She sipped her tea. "I always had the feeling that they wanted other kids, though."

"What were their names?" he asked. "Your parents, I mean."

"Marco and Dianna."

"You know," he said provocatively, "Dianna was the goddess of the hunt; she knew what she wanted and how to get it."

"My middle name is Dianna," Hanita said, winking at Vytas. She touched his hand that was now stroking her outer thigh. Her eyes melted like pools of chocolate as she gazed at him with sexual longing.

"Are your parents still in the south?" he asked.

"They vowed never to leave the south," she exclaimed, chuckling. "They absolutely hate the west."

"Such strong feelings."

Hanita waved him off that topic with a "You don't want to know" expression on her face. "But I love the west," she went on, thinking how much better it had seemed today than before.

"So what's your story?" she challenged, giving his strong hand a playful squeeze.

He leaned his head back slightly and sighed heavily. "Well," he began, "I also grew up in the south."

"Really?" she asked, squinting at him.

"Yes," he replied, nodding. "It's odd we never met."

"Hmm." She thought that over. "Why do you say that?"

"We have Alice in common," he reminded her. "We were bound to have run across each other while serving on the Confederation, but I wonder if Alice was keeping us apart."

She raised her eyebrows at him. "That's an interesting observation."

"I also wonder why we didn't run into each other at school," he added.

"I was mostly homeschooled," she offered. "Plus my parents traveled a lot for work, and I always had to tag along."

"That sounds like a difficult life for a child."

"True, it was." She thought this over. "But it was also interesting. I met many new people and saw the world." She was used to hiding the pain of her childhood behind a tough shell, but sitting here with Vytas, she could feel the cracks forming but still felt the need to hold back.

"Tell me more about you," she prodded, shaking off the memories.

He thought for a moment then said, "Well, you already know I have a sister, Alice." He did not enjoy talking about himself, so it was difficult for him to know what was worth sharing. "She is older than me, by the way."

"I was wondering," she said. "Would she consider you a good brother?"

"I certainly hope so," he exclaimed. He laughed, deep and loud. It was a natural and genuine laugh that put her at ease, and she laughed along with him.

"I'm really curious about your name," she confessed.

"Ah yes," Vytas said. "'Defender of the people,'" he explained. "I was named for my grandfather on my mother's side."

"It's such a strong, sexy name," she said breathlessly. "You seem to know a lot about the meaning behind names. Why is that?"

"That's the astronomer in me, I guess," he answered. "And Babica."

"Babica," Hanita repeated. "Your grandmother?"

"Yes," he answered, curious. "How did you know?"

She wasn't sure how she knew that. Was it a lucky guess? Or was it something else? She simply shrugged her shoulders and asked, "So your grandmother taught you a lot?"

He nodded, sipping his coffee. "I spend a lot of time with her studying mythology, and names play an important role in the stories."

He slipped his hand behind her knee and effortlessly pulled her closer to his body.

"Babica always seemed to know more than everyone else," he remembered. "The things she taught me have always stuck with me."

Hanita's left leg was now resting over his right thigh; her right knee touching his left knee. His bent left arm was still resting on the back of the bench. Vytas slid his hand further up her thigh and leaned in close. The fresh stubble on his face bit her skin as he gently grazed her neck and cheek until his lips were next to her ear.

"Let's get out of here," he whispered, his thick voice enveloping her body in quivering vibrations.

****

As they strolled through the darkness, they were the only two people enjoying the beauty after a spring storm had just moved through. The sidewalks and streets were still damp, and the air was filled with the aroma of fresh rain. She leaned her head against Vytas's strong shoulder as they held hands and continued talking.

"Why did you decide to take your mother's surname?" she asked.

He slid his free hand into his pocket. He was uncomfortable talking about his mother, but at the same time, he felt like he wanted to share everything with Hanita.

"My mother, Audra, passed away when I was very young," he started slowly. "She had gotten sick like so many others ..."

"Radiation?"

"Yes," he replied, sighing. "She was doing very important work that likely saved a lot of lives but ultimately ended hers too soon."

Hanita stopped to face Vytas and placed her hand on his chest. "Wait. Your mother is Audra Boyd," she stated.

He nodded and said, "Yes."

"*The* Audra Boyd?"

"Oh, you've heard of her?" He laughed.

"Wow." Hanita started walking again, leading him with her.

"Anyway, I wanted to honor her by taking her name," he finished.

"She was a force." She looked up at him and caught his eyes. "I would have loved to have met her."

He kept her gaze as they walked. "She would have loved you," he supposed out loud.

They continued in silence, thoughts racing about what could have been ... what may be yet to come. They arrived at Vytas's apartment building and climbed the steps to the main entrance. He opened the door and held it while Hanita walked through.

He lived on the fifth floor of a twelve-story building. Once inside, she immediately began surveying the room. It was dark except for the glimmer of the city, highlighting the upper portion of the furnishings just enough for her to navigate a few feet into the room.

She could feel him just behind her, closing the door. A soft illuminating glow slowly filled the room as he turned a knob by the front door. She turned to see that he was determining just the right amount of lighting before continuing in further.

"I wrote my thesis on your mother's work," she said, matter-of-factly.

"Really?" he responded.

"Her work in the Eastern Hemisphere was inspirational," she said with admiration. "She had a curious mind, and she was fearless." She began unbuttoning her jacket as she strolled into the apartment. "I can't stop thinking about the summit and what she would have had to say about it."

She looked around, getting a feel for his taste.

Vytas seemed far away, perhaps wondering the same thing. He placed his satchel on the dining table and then quietly entered the kitchen.

Noticing the uncomfortable silence, she decided to change the mood. "You're quite the decorator."

"Ha," he said, smirking. "What can I get you to drink?"

"Do you have wine?" She slid her arms out of the sleeves of her uniform jacket, revealing the standard white, button-down, long-sleeved shirt. She hung the jacket over a dining chair and unhooked the first two buttons on her blouse, very aware that he was watching her.

"Is red okay?"

"Mm-hmm," she assented, far away in thought. She was studying the room, moving her eyes over the furniture and the artwork on the walls. Every piece appeared to be carefully chosen, and yet there was no obvious theme. He was a man of eclectic taste.

He pulled two wine glasses from a cabinet, carefully selected a bottle of red wine from the rack, and uncorked it. He carried the wine and the glasses to the living room and placed them on the coffee table. He sat down on the sofa, which was placed directly across from glass doors that opened onto a small balcony.

He poured wine into both glasses and picked one up as he lounged into the corner of the sofa. He took a sip as he continued watching her scrutinize his collection of books, music, and photos on the tall, built-in cabinets. She moved so gracefully, silently. She imagined how exciting it would be to get to know and understand him. It would make their life together so much more stimulating.

"You haven't said anything about your father," she stated.

"He and I aren't close," he admitted, sipping his wine.

She reached around and unpinned her hair that was rolled neatly on her head. Brunette waves tumbled over her shoulders as she tousled her hair loose. She turned toward him, smiled, and then made her way over to the sofa.

"Do you want to talk about your father?" she asked as she picked up the other glass of wine and sat onto the cushion beside him.

He watched as she slipped off her shoes and tucked her legs up underneath her on the sofa. "I didn't realize security officers were wearing three-inch heals these days," he teased, avoiding her question.

She looked at him inquisitively. His right arm was resting on the back of the sofa, and he was still holding the glass of wine in his left hand. She placed her left hand on his resting forearm and stroked down onto the back of his hand. Reflexively, he rolled his hand, and their fingers laced together fluidly.

"It's a business casual day," she joked.

"Is that right?" he laughed. "So on business days, what do you wear?" He paused, waiting for her to respond.

"Actually, this is pretty normal for me," she confessed. "I mostly design, test, and implement security protocols, versus actually providing security."

"That's sounds much more interesting," he said. "Go on."

"Have you heard of a Cognitive Reliability Evaluation?" she asked.

He raised his eyebrow and thought, *What an odd question*. But at the same time, he was mad with curiosity. "No," he replied hesitantly, "but my interest is piqued."

"It's a process of detecting truthfulness versus deception in a subject by observing physiological and nonverbal cues while asking a series of questions," she explained.

"You mean lie detection?"

"Well," she responded, shaking her head as she sipped her wine, "it's more sophisticated than that."

"Then I guess the answer is no, I've never heard of …"

"C-R-E," she finished for him, setting down her wine glass. "Cognitive Reliability Evaluation."

"Why do you ask? Am I in trouble?"

"Well," she responded, scooting her body closer to his and leaning toward him. "That all depends on whether you're an honest man or not."

His eyes diverted to the v-shaped opening of her blouse that spread open, revealing a hint of her breasts.

"Eyes up here," she commanded. She pointed her right index and middle fingers toward her own eyes, leading his gaze upward.

He obeyed, grinning. "Are you going to work your voodoo on me now?" he asked with a laugh.

She nodded while a seductive grin formed on her lips. "I picked up a few tricks during the time I spent moving around with my parents," she said as she unlaced her fingers from his and turned his arm over on the back of the sofa, revealing the underside of his wrist.

She placed two fingers on his pulse and wrapped her thumb underneath. Her eyes remained fixed on his the whole time. "Do you really believe the Long Winter will happen?" she questioned.

"I do," he answered confidently.

"Tsk-tsk," she scolded, wagging her finger at him. "No talking, V."

"Oh, it's 'V' now, is it?" he huffed, grinning widely.

Judging by his pupil dilation and increased heart rate, she could tell that he enjoyed that she had already given him a nickname.

"This game is all about nonverbal cues, so no more talking," she chided, struggling to hold back her laughter.

He winked at her. "Got it."

Again she asked, "Do you believe the Long Winter is coming?"

She observed him closely before moving on. "Do you believe in fate?" she asked.

He stayed silent, patient, while she scrutinized him again. "I can tell that you definitely do believe in fate," she announced.

She was correct, of course, but he did not respond, obeying her previous command.

"Was it fate that brought us together on the same day we learned of the Long Winter?"

After a few moments, a sly smile formed on her lips. She appeared to have reached the conclusion she was hoping for.

"I just have one more question for you," she whispered, leaning closer.

His eyes followed as she slid her hand into her pants pocket, pulled out her closed fist, and held it in front of him.

"Does the word *pineapple* mean anything to you?" she said, breathing heavily. Stone-faced, she opened her hand revealing a sparkling pineapple tchotchke that she had plucked from his built-in shelving unit.

His eyes widened as they moved from her hand back up to her eyes. "Thief!" He roared, laughing.

She could no longer contain her laughter. "You're from the south for sure."

He enjoyed how playful she was. They continued to laugh for a moment, and then she placed the pineapple on the coffee table and picked up her glass of wine.

"I have one just like that, you know," she offered, as she motioned at the tchotchke. "It's so unique."

"Who gave it to you?" he asked.

"My favorite teacher," she remarked. "Her name was Saira. She always said, 'Everyone from the south must have a pineapple tchotchke.'"

Vytas nodded in agreement and added, "Babica told me that pineapples are an expression of welcome and symbolize friendship, hospitality, and warmth."

"That's true," Hanita agreed. "Saira also told me that whenever I move to a new place, the pineapple tchotchke should be the first thing I unpack."

"Saira sounds very wise."

"She was," Hanita remembered. She became still and far away as she thought of her teacher and how much she missed her. Saira had been such an important part of her life for so many years. Losing her was something she had never quite gotten over.

Vytas could sense that this was a difficult subject, so he quickly moved on to another topic. "So how do you know Alice?"

"I was in charge of the security detail for her lab," Hanita answered. "That's how we met. We quickly became friends; Alice is just wonderful."

Vytas nodded his head in agreement, smiling warmly.

They talked and drank wine for hours. Vytas could feel the weight pulling on his eyelids. Before he allowed himself to fully succumb to fatigue, he gently brushed the hair from Hanita's face and stared into her sleepy, dark eyes.

He realized he was falling in love with her.

****

Vytas's eyes sprung open as his head launched off the pillow with a gasp. He was confused and disoriented for a moment. His eyes searched the room, left and right, for clues. He had fallen asleep on the sofa in his living room. He yawned and began to stretch.

Just then, he realized Hanita was there with him, her head and upper body lying on his chest, still asleep. His right arm was around her back, and his hand rested on her right shoulder. He smiled, comforted by the feel of her body against his. He remembered now. They had been talking late into the night and must have fallen asleep on the sofa.

He brought his other arm around and squeezed her closer, inhaling the fragrance of cherries and pomegranates in her hair. She stirred in his arms, moaning sleepily and squeezing him back.

It was morning. The sun was piercing the horizon with shards of light that sliced through the city buildings. Shadows formed in the room, creating elongated shapes from the slatted railing around the small balcony.

"What time is it?" she wondered, pushing her body up and rubbing her eyes.

"I don't know … early."

"I'm going down the hall," she announced as she stood up. "Be right back." She turned and bounced around the sofa and then out of the room.

"I'll make coffee," he called out as she closed the door to the guest bathroom in the hallway.

****

Vytas poured two cups of coffee and then returned to the living room. Hanita was standing in front of the glass doors, framed by the glow of the sunrise. She was admiring the view when she felt his body against hers and gently leaned into him. He brought his arm around in front of her and handed her the coffee mug.

As she took the mug from his hand, he slipped his arm around her shoulders. She placed her hand on his forearm and gently stroked his skin. They stood there in silence for a few moments, sipping coffee.

Then she turned to face him. She set her mug on the shelf, took the mug from his hand, and positioned it next to hers. She placed her hands on his chest and slowly started to unbutton his shirt.

Looking into his eyes, she purred, "Do you have to be anywhere this morning?" Her hands moved to the next button.

"No," he replied softly as he placed his hands around her waist. "Not before ten."

"Good." Her hands moved to the next button, and she gently pushed him backward, toward the sofa. She tugged at the bottom of his shirt, pulling the wrinkled ends from his blue jeans. She freed the last buttons and then brushed the shirt away from his chest, her fingers moving over tufted skin on his abdomen and defined pecs.

They reached the sofa. Hanita nudged him to sit down and then climbed onto his lap, her thighs straddling him. She placed her hands on his shoulders, under his shirt, and then caressed his neck as she leaned toward him. He tilted his head back, their lips parting as they met.

Her fingers moved up and spread through his hair as she pressed into his mouth deeper, again and again. Then she pulled away, lingering on his lower lip, letting it slide between her teeth. His eyes were closed as he savored their first kiss.

She started to unbutton her blouse. He watched as she revealed a lacy pink bra. His hands prowled up her sides and felt her breasts. Then he gently lifted her from his lap and laid her onto the sofa on her back. His left knee pressed into the cushion as he slowly slipped out of his unbuttoned shirt, tilting his shoulders left and right.

She reached her hand up, slipping her fingers under the waistband of his blue jeans, and then pulled him down onto her body. She wrapped her legs around his hips, and they melted together.

Chapter 3

Hanita was perched at her workstation in the lab, dutifully tapping away on her keyboard. She had slipped out of her three-inch heels and assumed the tree pose, standing on her left leg with her right leg bent, pressing her right foot into the side of her left thigh. She had some work to catch up on before day two of the summit resumed today.

She stretched her back and placed her right foot onto the cold tile while examining her work. Then she raised her arms high above her head and arched her back. Resuming the tree pose, she tugged at the hem of her jacket to straighten it, feeling glad that she wore a uniform to work so no one would realize she was in the same clothes as yesterday.

A hint of fragrance that had been lingering on her shirt collar was released and wafted into the air. She breathed in the mystical aroma of fiery incense and crushed spices, and her thoughts returned to Vytas. Her eyes drifted shut as she dreamed of his lips on her neck.

"You have the same goofy look on your face as my brother."

Alice's voice pulled Hanita back to reality. She opened her eyes to see her friend peering at her from over the monitor. "Good morning, Alice," she sang as she began typing again.

"Ugh," Alice groaned, folding her arms tightly across her chest. She rolled her eyes and then walked around the tall desk to stand next to Hanita. She had placed her elbow on Hanita's workstation and rested her chin in her hand.

"You weren't at the gym this morning," she prodded, playfully nudging Hanita's arm.

Hanita was staring at the monitor in front of her and smirked, offering no explanation.

Alice was unusually quiet. She wasn't writing in her notebook; she was just hovering at Hanita's workstation and drumming her fingers.

"Clearly there's something on your mind," Hanita deduced. She punctuated her work with a press of a button and then turned to face Alice. "Are you asking me for details?"

"No," Alice exclaimed, waving her off. "God, no. That would be gross."

"Well, then what is it?"

"I saw Kyle yesterday," Alice said, "after Vytas's presentation."

"Kyle—that's your college friend, right?"

She nodded and said, "He looked great. I invited him to have dinner with me."

"So how did it go?"

Alice squinted and shook her head. "It hasn't happened yet," she answered. "We're going to try for one night this week while he's in town for the summit."

Hanita placed her hand on her friend's forearm and squeezed. "Alice, you don't seem happy."

"It was just strange," she admitted, looking far away. Then looking back, she added, "He was my friend while we were in college … but seeing him yesterday, it's like I was seeing him in a different way."

Alice checked the time on the monitor over Hanita's shoulder. "We have to go," she said. "The summit starts in ten minutes."

Hanita pressed the keys on her keyboard to lock the workstation. "To be continued," she teased as they hurried out of the lab.

****

Vytas was already at the podium on stage when Alice and Hanita entered the auditorium. He was sipping his water when he saw them. He shared a knowing glance and subtle wave with Hanita before she turned to climb the steps to seats higher up and farther back then yesterday. There were no seats available closer to the stage.

He checked the clock and decided it was time to begin. He switched on the microphone clipped onto his shirt collar. "Good morning, everyone," he began. "I hope you all had time to review the material from yesterday and that you arrived today ready to get to work." He listened as the murmuring grew.

"I know you're anxious to get started," he said, signaling for them to be patient and then waiting for the voices to subside before moving on.

"We're going to do something a little different today," he continued. "You may have noticed numbers on your seat backs when you were sitting down. We're going to split into thirty groups of ten. The number on your seat back indicates your group number.

"The objective is for you to workshop the problem presented to you in yesterday's kickoff," he explained. "Hopefully, by combining you all randomly, you will challenge each other and brainstorm.

"This will be more productive than trying to work this out in a group of three hundred, don't you agree?" he asked, nodding to the audience.

"Okay, so we have thirty conference rooms in the building that have been reserved for our summit." He walked to the left side of the stage and motioned to a whiteboard hanging on the wall below the stage floor. "Here, you will find your conference room assignment, based on the group number you were assigned."

He checked the time on the wall clock. "It's just a little past ten hundred hours," he verified. "Let's try to get to your assigned room by ten thirty, choose a team leader, and get started."

Some people began to stand and move toward the auditorium aisles and steps. He motioned for them to wait. "Before you go, let me add, we want you to be as productive as possible today. Lunch will be brought in to the conference rooms, and I will be checking in on all of you during the day.

"We will work until sixteen hundred or until your group develops a detailed action plan.

"Okay, let's get started," he said, formally dismissing them. "Team leaders, turn in your proposals back here by sixteen hundred. We will begin discussing them tomorrow."

****

Hanita re-entered the auditorium at fifteen thirty hours. Her group had just finished their proposal, and she was eager to turn it in and see Vytas. He was standing in front of the stage with his back to her as she approached. Someone else was handing over their document so she waited for her turn. She wondered what the confederation would say if their affair was discovered.

He had set up a table to receive the submissions and was neatly fastening the pages together before laying them in a stack. As the other representative turned and walked away from them, Hanita placed her hand on Vytas's shoulder and stepped beside him. He looked over and saw her.

He scooped his arm around her and pulled her close against his body. "I've missed you," he said in his low, smoky voice. They shared an intimate, wet kiss before slowly pulling their bodies apart. She pushed her stray bangs behind her ear as she looked around, wondering if they had been seen.

"Are you planning to review those all by yourself?" she asked.

He sighed heavily as he eyed the large stack of documents on the table in front of them. "It's going to be a late night for me, I'm afraid," he confirmed.

"Would you like some help?"

"I would love some help," he said, smiling.

"It's a date," she confirmed, squeezing his arm. "I have some work to finish up, so why don't I meet you at your place?"

"I'll make dinner," he agreed. "Eighteen hundred?"

She nodded. "I'll bring beer."

****

Vytas was seated on the bed, wearing only his boxer shorts. The bedsheets were still strewn about and covered with separate stacks of papers. He was holding a document in front of his naked chest, reading in the dim light of his bedroom. His left leg was dangling off the side of the bed while his right leg was folded underneath his body.

"I found another one, babe," he called out, still reading.

A moment later, Hanita appeared in the doorway carrying two pilsner glasses of rich, golden-colored beer topped by a thin layer of froth. "How many is that now?" she asked.

She was wearing one of Vytas's shirts. The sleeves were rolled up in bulky masses around her forearms, and the shirttail hung to her mid-thigh. The shirt was open except for two buttons fastened just above her belly button, revealing bikini-style black panties. She glided onto the bed and handed him one of the glasses.

Vytas sipped from the glass as he counted. "Twenty-one," he confirmed.

"So that's good, right," she said. "Seventy percent of the Confederation agrees."

"They agree more-or-less anyway." Vytas looked at the document piles on the bed. They had read through all of the submissions and sorted them into six stacks, based on the general idea behind the proposal. One stack had four proposals, another stack had two proposals. There were three outlier proposals that were unlike any of the others.

And then there was one pile of twenty-one similar proposals. Vytas laid his hand on the heap of papers. "The idea that is going to save us is in this stack," he confirmed.

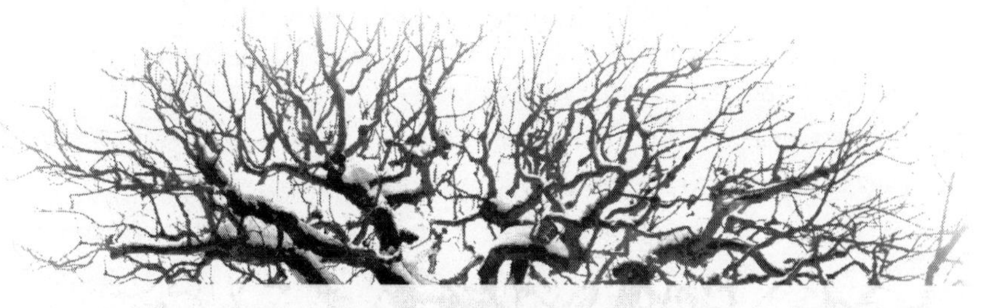

Chapter 4

"Are we still on for lunch today?" Alice asked.

"Um," Hanita replied, hesitating. Then she shrugged her shoulders and conceded. "Sure. It's Wednesday, after all."

They had just left the lab and were making their way to the auditorium once again for day three of the summit. The halls were bustling with the normal activity, and then, of course, there were all of the visitors adding additional chaos. Hanita was looking forward to a chance to sit down with Alice and talk. She had so many questions that she didn't dare ask but was hopeful that her friend would open up about.

"I had to ask." Alice playfully nudged Hanita on the shoulder. "Maybe you would stand me up for my brother?"

Hanita had considered doing just that. Something had been weighing on her the last couple of days and she was afraid their regular lunch date was the perfect opportunity to unload. "Not a chance."

There was a sign posted just inside. They joined the small crowd gathered around it, reading it over. It was asking the attendees to sit with their workshop groups today.

Hanita surveyed the room and noticed that the auditorium had been divided into thirty sections, marked by numbered seats. She located her group's section. "I'm over there," she said to Alice, pointing across the room.

"Okay," Alice responded. "I'm on this side. See you later?"

They shared one last glance before walking off and taking their seats in their assigned sections.

****

"We meet again," Vytas announced to the audience from behind the podium, smiling warmly. "After reviewing all of the proposals yesterday evening, I'm happy to report that we have a common theme."

He stepped out from behind the podium where he had set up a table to hold the stacks of proposals. He placed his hand over the largest stack. "Twenty-one of our teams proposed we survive the Long Winter in some form of stasis," he announced, making air quotes with his fingers.

"Today, we will explore these various proposals," he continued. "This will be somewhat of an open debate. Each group has a team leader that you selected yesterday. The team leaders will be the spokesperson of each group during the debate."

Vytas sat on the edge of the table and folded his hands across his body. "Shall we begin?" he asked. Hearing no objections, he continued, "Good. I'd like to start by letting the groups summarize how they came to their conclusion."

He lifted the document from the top of the largest stack and scanned the front page. "Group seven," he announced. "Would the team leader stand, introduce yourself, and open the discussion?"

Vytas lifted his eyes from the document he was holding in front of himself and noticed someone stand up on his right side. He motioned to one of his assistants to bring a microphone to the new speaker and then he returned his gaze to the woman.

It was Hanita, standing with her group. She reached out to the assistant and accepted the microphone. Vytas thought back to yesterday when she turned in the proposal from her group. It never dawned on him at the time that she was acting as the team leader for her group, and he never checked the group number written on top of the page.

She winked at Vytas, and he lowered his head, smiling as he realized that she had kept that secret last night.

She switched on the microphone and then casually waved at the audience. "Hello, everyone," she said. "My name is Agent Hanita Michaels. I'm an architectural engineer and head of security operations in this building."

The group responded, some by saying or waving hello, others only nodding.

"In group seven, we started to work out the problem by asking ourselves what we would need to survive the Long Winter," she began. She held the microphone in her left hand so she could gesture with her dominant right hand as she spoke. "The most important things are food, water, and shelter." She counted out the items on her fingers as she listed them.

"We all heard on Monday that these critical items will be at risk when the Long Winter arrives." She stretched out her hand as she glanced around the auditorium. The other attendees nodded in agreement.

"For five years — perhaps longer — the surface will be under a sheet of ice and a heavy blanket of snow. We won't have a food source," she went on. "Vegetation will be frozen; fruit trees and vegetable-bearing plants will not be producing; livestock and other wildlife will die.

"There will likely be chemical pollutants raining down, so even if we could brave the elements to collect snow to melt for water, it won't be safe to drink.

"And then there's the issue of shelter," she continued. "Some structures will likely be destroyed during the Long Winter, and people will be at risk for exposure as a result.

"So then we asked ourselves, how could we provide these basic necessities to approximately three billion people for roughly five years?"

She paused as she looked around the room. "We could begin stockpiling food and water, but how much will we need?" she asked. "A lot, right," she responded to her own question, nodding. "Where would we store this much food and water? And can we store it safely?

"How would we get these supplies to three billion people during the Long Winter?"

She shook her head. "We just kept reaching the same conclusion: We can't."

The room responded with an ebb and flow of whispers, murmurs, gasps, and groans.

"Thank you, Hanita," Vytas said, as he shared a brief glimpse with her before she took her seat again.

Then, addressing the room, Vytas said, "Group seven has provided many excellent points to consider. These are all very real possibilities." He scanned the room, confirming that he had everyone's attention. "Would anyone else like to add anything?"

In his peripheral vision, he noticed someone standing from the left side of the room. A figure from the left of the stage emerged from the shadows, carrying a microphone.

"Good day," the man said to the room. "My name is Dr. Louis Wong. I'm the chief of cardiothoracic surgery at Eastern University Hospital, and I'm representing group twelve.

"We discussed a lot of the same challenges that Agent Michaels described," Dr. Wong began. "We thought about constructing a housing complex, if you will, that could contain everyone, in multiple buildings, but in the same area." Dr. Wong covered the microphone and bent down as one of his team members whispered something to him. He nodded in response and then continued addressing the room.

"This is also where we could store supplies like food, water, clothing, medicine, and the like."

Dr. Wong raised his hand and pointed his index finger up. "But there are flaws with this idea," he continued. "We would have to ration the food and water. But what if the rations provided to a family or group are depleted? What will happen?

"Violence may break out. Rations could be stolen from others or from the main cache. There will be chaos," he hypothesized.

"Another flaw is there will be illness. We will have medical supplies, of course, but how do we reach the sick? How will they reach the medical personnel?"

"Viruses will spread quickly among groups, infecting too many to properly treat. How many people will die?" Dr. Wong asked softly.

Vytas stood from his leaning post and stepped toward the front of the stage. "Thank you, Dr. Wong," he said.

Dr. Wong nodded back, switched off the microphone, and took his seat.

"Anyone else?" Vytas asked the room as he looked around, waiting for someone to stand.

"I would like to add something," a voice called out from the back of the room.

One of the assistants jogged up the steps to the silhouette in the back of the room and passed off a microphone.

"Hello," the gravelly voice announced. "I'm Dr. Steven White, head of cancer research in this building, and I'm representing group nineteen."

Dr. White cleared his throat before continuing, "It sounds like several groups, including ours, went through the same process in our breakout session yesterday.

"Group nineteen desperately tried to figure out a way for humanity to ride out the Long Winter. But let's face it," he demanded. "Only 40 percent of the population survived a major extinction-level event when Jupiter exploded. What makes you think we will survive this one?"

The room was awash of conversations that rumbled from one side of the room to the next in waves. It was impossible to make any sense out of what was being said.

Vytas, surprised by Dr. White's comments, turned and walked back to the table. He located the proposal from group nineteen, one of the outliers. As he skimmed the page, he remembered that this group had proposed something pretty radical.

"Dr. White," Vytas said loudly, attempting to overpower the other voices. "Shh-shh," he said to the room, motioning for silence as he approached the front of the stage again. "Dr. White," he repeated.

"Yes, Dr. Boyd?"

Vytas was holding the submission in front of him. "Group nineteen proposed a lottery to decide who would survive and who would die, correct?"

The room erupted in shouting and scoffing at Dr. White's conclusion, especially within his own group. In an act of munity, a couple of his team members tried to take the microphone from the burly Dr. White, but he would not relinquish control.

From the left side of the room, someone shouted, "*Selective* survival?"

Vytas stood tall and shook his head emphatically as he gestured with his right hand. "Let's not go there yet," he responded. "Let's focus first on survival for all of us."

Dr. Wong handed his microphone off to the spokesperson for group nine seated a few rows behind him.

Vytas, having witnessed the exchange, made an announcement. "Everyone, let's please quiet down and take your seats." His voice boomed through the auditorium, overpowering all the other noise. The room began to fall silent again as everyone turned their attention back to their speaker. He waited as the people quieted down and then motioned to the new speaker.

"Hi, good morning," she said. "My name is Elizabeth Martinez. I'm the district attorney up North, and I represent group nine.

"We hypothesized that if we could somehow hibernate during the Long Winter, this would be our best chance for survival." Elizabeth, unlike the other speakers, looked directly at Vytas when she spoke.

"How do you propose three billion people hibernate?" Vytas asked, making air-quotes with his fingers again.

Elizabeth nodded to Vytas. "We have some scientists in our group who read about cryogenics," she continued. "We believe this could be a possible solution."

"Thank you, Ms. Martinez," Vytas responded, as he checked the time. "I think this is a good stopping point. Let's break for lunch and meet back here at thirteen hundred to continue the discussion."

****

Vytas exited the stage and watched as Kyle made his way down from his seat near the back of the auditorium. As he approached, Vytas extended his right hand.

"Kyle," he said. "It's good to see you again."

Kyle grasped Vytas's hand, taken aback at first that he remembered him. "I didn't think you remembered me. We only met the one time …"

"When you and my sister, Alice, graduated from college," Vytas finished his sentence for him, smiling and squeezing Kyle's hand tightly.

"That's right," Kyle remembered. "I ran into Alice on Monday," he added, stammering nervously after saying her name. "We're hoping to have some time this week to catch up."

"I think that would be a great idea," Vytas agreed, releasing Kyle's hand. He turned his body and motioned for his colleague to follow him. They stepped away from the exit door, where the other attendees were moving around, and walked toward the stage, where it was more private.

"I wanted to ask you for a favor," Vytas began.

"Sure," Kyle said, folding his arms across his chest.

"I've been following your work. Most of the scientific community considers your theories controversial, but I find them interesting."

Kyle lowered his head and did not respond. He was aware of what other scientists were saying about his experiments.

"Look," Vytas continued, leaning down slightly in order to meet Kyle's eyes. "I don't share the same opinions as my colleagues. I wanted to ask you if you would speak to the group after lunch."

"I don't know if that's such a good idea," Kyle said.

Vytas put his hand on Kyle's shoulder. Motioning toward the auditorium with his head, Vytas urged, "They need to hear what you have to say."

****

Hanita could feel dozens of pairs of eyes staring at them as they sat quietly scooping up bites of food, like two soldiers in a mess hall. She and Alice had managed to secure a high table in the cafeteria on the lower level of the building. Wednesday was their regular lunch date, and they decided the summit should not change that. Besides, Hanita was hoping to uncover answers to the questions swirling through her mind. But how? She couldn't actually interrogate her friend.

Alice seemed unfazed by the awkward silence, no doubt lost in her own thoughts. But Hanita couldn't stop wondering why she would have kept so many secrets from her. They had been friends for years now, but Alice had never mentioned that she had a brother, that he was on the Confederation, that he was leading this summit. Hanita pierced a chunk of meat with her fork and jammed it in her mouth, unable to make eye contact with her friend.

She wanted to ask Alice about her mother, Audra Boyd. The work that she was involved in was so groundbreaking, and she was one Hanita's idols. Why hadn't they talked about her before? Hanita couldn't understand why Alice wouldn't mention being related to her. Was she too proud to bring it up? Was it too painful to talk about? Or was there another reason? Did it have to do with their father?

Hanita was naturally suspicious of everyone until she could gather enough information to make an informed decision, and she had decided long ago about Alice. She loved Alice like a sister. She wasn't used to having doubts about someone she had trusted for so many years. It left a foul taste in her mouth, like something you wanted to spit out and scrape away.

"I thought Vytas had lost control of the room," Alice whispered, cutting through the tension. Alice enjoyed the quiet, but it was unusual for Hanita to not be talking. Alice could sense something was up with her.

"It did look that way," Hanita responded, looking down as she pushed the food around on her plate.

"But he has always had a way of wrangling an audience back under control."

Hanita nodded her head as she scooped a bite of food into her mouth. "He's quite impressive."

"I would have to agree with that." She poked at the last bits of food on the plate in front of her. Suddenly, she stopped and grew very serious. "I hope you're not put off that I never introduced you to him," she blurted out.

Hanita dropped her fork and picked up the napkin lying across her lap, raising it to her mouth. Her brow was furrowed as she met Alice's eyes. She wanted to shout, "I'm not put off; I'm fucking angry." But she bit her cheek and held in the words behind the napkin.

"I just hope you understand that I don't think about fix-ups," she admitted.

"Alice," Hanita said softly as she lowered the napkin to her lap. She paused as she met Alice's eyes and felt the burden of betrayal lift away. She saw, not an adversary, but a friend staring back at her. Hanita reached across the table and touched Alice's arm. "It's fine."

She had already learned so much about Alice through Vytas after only just meeting him on Monday. In contrast to Alice, he was very open. The answers to all of Hanita's questions would be answered soon enough, so there was no reason to jeopardize her friendship with Alice by trying to pry information out of her.

"I've just been thinking about the summit," Hanita lied. "It's a lot to take in."

"Welcome to the Confederation," Alice replied, laughing.

Still one question lingered in the back of Hanita's mind: *Why were Alice and Vytas so different? What happened to them*?

****

"Welcome back," Vytas said, smiling. "I hope everyone had a good lunch." He listened as some in the audience groaned, while others laughed.

"Before the break, Elizabeth Martinez from group nine broached the topic of cryogenics," Vytas reminded them.

"How can we make cryogenics work?" The room was silent, pondering Vytas's question.

"I know we all have a lot more questions." Vytas strode out from behind the podium. "So I thought we would start with, what is cryogenics?

"I would like to turn the floor over to my colleague, Dr. Kyle Weber, a leading expert in this field."

Alice glanced to the left side of the room as Kyle jogged up the steps and onto the stage.

Vytas removed the microphone from his collar and placed it on the podium. He extended his right hand and placed his left hand on Kyle's shoulder. They shook hands as they passed each other on the stage, and Kyle stepped up to the podium.

He nervously clipped the microphone to his collar and cleared his throat. "So let me begin by first clarifying that what we're talking about is cryonics versus cryogenics." His voice fractured as he addressed the room full of three hundred experts. He purposefully kept his eyes fixed on the podium, the floor, or one of the walls. Not making eye contact made it easier for him to communicate.

He never mastered how much eye contact is too much or too little. Avoiding it all together was best for him, though it did seem to make other people uncomfortable. Only his close friends and family really understood; they didn't take it personally.

"Cryogenics is the production and behavior of materials at very low temperatures." He spoke with a peculiar way of enunciation, mechanical and trembling. "In contrast, cryonics has typically meant the low-temperature freezing and storage of a human corpse with the hope that resurrection may be possible in the future.

"We have been working quite a bit with cryonics over the last decade and are making strides." He began to relax as he stroked his fingers across the podium, focusing on the feel of the wood grain and letting the audience slip away into the darkness.

"Speaking in terms of humanity and life, this process of cryonics was previously only successful at the cellular level, such as embryos that were frozen until such time as they could be implanted into a host, resulting in the live birth of babies." He spoke about the process with little emotion, as if he were talking about machine parts stored in a warehouse, used to replace broken equipment.

"We have had limited success with live tissue, such as human organs." He shifted his weight from side to side as he spoke. "We used to have time limits on when a human organ had to be transplanted into a recipient's body after the donor body expired. This resulted in viable tissue either going to waste because we ran out of time or being used for scientific research because there was no available host to receive the transplanted organ.

"But recently, we successfully froze human tissue after the organ donor's death using cryonics and then later brought that tissue out of cold storage and successfully implanted it into a live host."

A skeptical voice from the audience called out, "Have you brought back a human being from cryonic storage?"

Kyle's eyes drifted up from the podium. The audience, once disguised within the darkness, was visible again. Sweat began to bead on his forehead as he responded, "No."

Alice could feel his pain as he nervously fidgeted, in an attempt to dodge the audience outburst. It was like watching a wounded animal trying to escape a trap.

She wanted to rescue him, so she tossed him a lifeline. "Do you think it's possible?" she shouted, calling above all the other voices.

Kyle turned toward the sound of Alice's voice and saw her standing in front of her seat. He felt safe again, as if she had wrapped him in a blanket that shielded him from the attack.

"Yes," he answered confidently. "Yes, I do."

Vytas approached the podium and said, "Thanks, Kyle. You can take your seat."

Kyle started to walk away, but then Vytas grabbed his arm. "Wait," Vytas said, as he plucked the microphone from his shirt collar. "I'll need this." He smiled and squeezed Kyle's shoulder before turning back toward center stage.

Kyle was walking down the steps as Vytas moved on. "So for argument's sake, let's assume cryonics is an option. How would we do it?"

The audience murmured and fidgeted in their seats. Vytas could see that he was getting a lot of confused looks and decided to rephrase his question.

"Not the *process* of putting a human being into cryonic storage," he clarified. "That will be Dr. Weber's job." Vytas's comment resulted in much-needed laughter after the anger and tension from the morning discussion.

"No pressure, Kyle," a voice from the audience shouted.

The laughter subsided then Vytas jammed his hands in his pockets and walked across the stage to the left. He looked at the stage as he shuffled his feet and thought out loud, "If we were to freeze three billion human beings using cryonics ..." He stopped and looked out at the audience. "Where would we put them?"

The audience was silent. Vytas waited for a volunteer to speak, but no one accepted the challenge. He returned to the small table placed in front of the podium and leafed through the tall stack of similar proposals.

Finally stopping, Vytas turned to the audience and declared, "Group twenty-one. We haven't heard from you, but as I recall, you did have an idea." He was holding their proposal in his hands as he strode out to the front of the stage.

One of the assistants ran up the steps on the right side of the room. The spokesperson for group twenty-one stood and adjusted his slacks before accepting the microphone from the assistant.

"Hi, everyone," he said. "My name is Dr. Ron Smith; I'm an aerodynamics engineer. So," he began, taking in a deep breath, "our idea in group twenty-one is to build a facility to hold three billion hibernating humans." Ron spoke quickly and analytically.

"All in one facility?" a voice near the front asked.

"How big would it have to be?" another person asked.

Ron laughed as he bobbed on his heels. "Roughly sixty billion square feet, by our calculations."

The audience groaned and squirmed in their seats as muffled skepticism was building.

Vytas raised his hand in front of his body to calm the group as Dr. Smith started to take his seat. "Hold on, Dr. Smith," he said, motioning for him to stand again. "You are assuming that everyone will accept the option to hibernate in cryonic storage."

Dr. Smith raised his shoulders and looked back at Vytas pragmatically. "Well, yes, "he responded.

"Does everyone agree with that assumption?" Vytas asked.

The room began to rumble with outbursts from all around.

"Let's take this one at a time," Vytas said, motioning for everyone to settle down. "Who wants to go first?"

Several hands shot up. Vytas pointed at a new speaker on his right. One of the assistants ran a microphone up as he made his way to the end of the aisle. He switched on the microphone, and it made a loud squeak.

"Sorry," he said, grimacing. "Didn't mean for that to happen. Is this better?" he asked, laughing.

A glint from the left caught Vytas's eyes; it was the overhead light reflecting on Alice's glasses. He noticed that she also had her hand up and motioned to one of his assistants to take a microphone to her so she could speak next.

"Hi, I'm Dr. Jeff Bolton, group ten. Our spokesperson gave me permission to speak. I feel strongly that we need to consider multiple locations, and here's why: We don't really know how bad the surface will be during the Long Winter.

"Dr. Boyd painted a pretty grim picture, but one thing you left out," he said, looking directly at Vytas, "are the projectiles in the dust cloud.

"If we're all snuggled up in our tin cans in one facility, and we get hit by a meteor …" He stopped and made a clicking noise out of the side of his mouth. "Well, that would be all she wrote for us."

The woman next to Dr. Bolton stood up and leaned in toward the microphone. "I wanted to add that there's also a chance the facility could experience some other type of emergency, like a power failure."

"Exactly," Dr. Bolton added. "There's any number of things that could happen while we're sleeping," he said. "It's smarter to split us up. It gives us a better chance of survival." Dr. Bolton clicked off the microphone he was holding and took his seat.

"Alice, please stand," Vytas said, motioning to his sister.

"Hello," Alice said as she stood in front of her seat. "I'm Dr. Alice Wallace. I'm the head of bioresearch here in the west. I have a lab in this building and am the spokesperson for group six.

"This is a topic that we explored in some detail," Alice continued. "Although we did not specifically discuss cryonics," she added, gesturing toward Vytas, "let's assume for the sake of argument that we did.

"We strongly believe that a large number of people will decide against cryonics, whether that be due to fear or religious beliefs or skepticism that the Long Winter will even happen. But it's impossible to estimate just how many.

"There are, however, other estimates we can discuss. Roughly 5 percent of the current population is sixty-five years of age or older. Considering the health issues, how many of them would decide against cryonics?

"There is the possibility that their bodies would be unable to handle the process of going into or coming out of the cryonic state," Alice continued. "So should age be an exclusionary issue?

"We also have a large population of terminally ill who will die before the Long Winter is expected to end. But what about those who may become sick between now and its onset?" Alice asked. "Will they choose cryonics, only to face death soon after waking up? Will they survive the process?

"On the opposite end of the spectrum are the children," Alice went on. "How young is too young for cryonics? Can the brain of an infant that isn't fully developed withstand the process?

"These are difficult things to consider," Alice concluded, "but we must."

Elizabeth Martinez stood in front of her seat, still holding her microphone. "I would also like to mention our criminal population," she interjected. "That's approximately 8 percent of the population."

"What do you suggest we do with them?" Hanita asked.

Elizabeth turned to her left to face Hanita, now standing amongst her group. "Why would we exclude the elderly and sick …"

"And children," another voice chimed in.

"And children," Elizabeth acknowledged, "but not the prison population? That's my point."

"Are you saying all prisoners should be turned away, or just the really nasty ones?" Hanita retorted.

Elizabeth threw up her hands and took her seat as strong comments emanated from the audience in support of both sides of the argument.

Noticing that Hanita was still standing, Vytas attempted to unruffle the wound-up opinions so she may continue.

Unable to wait any longer, Hanita made her last point very loudly. "All life is precious," she announced. "We shouldn't be so dismissive." She then switched off the microphone and took her seat.

Dr. Wong and Alice both proclaimed their agreement with Hanita's point. Others in the audience also joined in. The tension around this topic was boiling over and needed to be brought under control.

"Everyone," Vytas called out, "let's take our seats and quiet down." He watched and waited patiently as the arguments concluded. "Thank you all for your honesty on this topic," he added. "I know this is very difficult, and many of you feel very passionately, but I think we should table this discussion for now."

Vytas scanned the audience and found Dr. Smith from group twenty-one. Motioning in his direction, Vytas began, "I'd like to return to Dr. Smith's idea around how we would house or store the survivors." He brought his hands together in front of his body; fingers interlaced, he raised his closed hands up under his chin, deep in thought as he walked slowly across the stage.

"If we're able to use cryonics to freeze the hosts, this would mean they'd be in some sort of hibernation chamber." He looked into the audience and added, "Correct?" His question was met with nods and muffled approval.

"Dr. Smith," Vytas announced, "would the facility be above ground or below ground?"

Dr. Smith stood in front of his chair and switched on the microphone he was still holding. "Below ground, Dr. Boyd," he answered. "That would be our recommendation, given the anticipated conditions on the surface."

"Dr. Bolton," Vytas said, pointing into the audience with his right hand as he lowered his left hand to his side. "What are your thoughts regarding multiple, underground facilities to house the hibernation chambers? Is this a possibility?"

"In a word, yes." Dr. Bolton was now also standing speaking into his microphone. "We discussed this option in our group and believe we have time to construct these facilities before the Long Winter arrives.

"However," Dr. Bolton went on, "this will be a massive project. I … we," he corrected, looking at his team members, "know that it will take cooperation and collaboration from everyone in order to get it done."

Vytas tilted his head back and raised one eyebrow in agreement with Dr. Bolton's words. He inhaled deeply as he turned and continued walking toward the other side of the stage, searching carefully for his next words. The audience waited patiently, quietly, and collectively holding their breath as they watched his every step.

Stopping abruptly to face the room, Vytas asked, "Are you all as exhausted as I am?"

The representatives responded in laughter, feeling as though they could breathe again.

"I think we've all heard enough for one day," he went on. "Let's end a little early today and resume in the morning." With that, he switched off the microphone clipped to his shirt collar, removed it, and laid it on the podium. The room filled with voices and footsteps as the representatives filed out of the auditorium.

****

Hanita was quiet as she walked out of the building with Vytas. It had been a long day, and she had let Elizabeth Martinez rile her up. It wasn't the first time. She had encountered Elizabeth in her past and was familiar with her beliefs. She wasn't a fan.

"Today was pretty intense," Vytas whispered as he slipped his arm around her shoulder. "How are you feeling?"

His embrace was warm and comforting. She could feel all the weight of the anger she'd been experiencing lift away. With Vytas, she felt lighter and safe. His arm around her was like a cloak of protection, shielding her from all that was happening around them and from what was coming.

She leaned her head on his chest and breathed deep as she wrapped her arms around his waist. "I'm better now," she murmured, squeezing him tightly.

"Do you want to talk about it?"

"Maybe later," she said. "Right now, I just want to forget."

They walked on quietly for a few minutes before Vytas asked, "How do you know Elizabeth Martinez?"

Hanita looked up at him with her crooked smile, meeting his eyes and searching for clues. "What makes you think I know her?" she asked. *How could he know?* she thought.

He turned away, looking straight ahead as they continued walking. "I sense there's a history between you," he replied. Then looking back into her eyes, he added, "Only someone you know could get you that angry."

"You think you know me that well already," she replied, laughing and digging her fingers into his side.

He flinched at her prodding. "Yes, I do," he admitted. They were quiet for the rest of the walk to his apartment.

****

"I'm glad I caught you," Alice said, breathing heavily.

"Alice," Kyle said, relieved to see a friendly face. He was eager to leave the building, having not enjoyed being put on the spot today. He didn't really care why she was glad to catch up to him but hoped that she could ease his mind.

"I think we should coordinate our projects," she suggested.

"Oh?" Kyle was curious but still, he was just more interested in being able to spend time with Alice. "What are you working on?"

She looked around at the other conference members passing by, gathering around in their own conversations. She could hear them whispering about cryonics and stepped closer to Kyle in an attempt to create a barrier between him and their words.

She leaned closer and put her hand on his arm. "Let's talk over dinner," she said softly and began leading him through the crowded hallway.

"Sure," he replied.

"I'm buying."

****

"How long has it been?" Alice asked Kyle. They had decided to grab dinner at an outdoor café nearby. Having shed their lab coats at the office, they looked like a couple out on a date.

"How long?" Kyle repeated, looking puzzled.

She had nearly forgotten how socially awkward he was. He didn't always understand social situations or common forms of shorthand communication between close friends. It was easy for him to misunderstand or not recognize the feelings or reactions of others.

For this reason, he had a hard time making friends. He appeared to have a disregard for other people's feelings and sometimes came across as insensitive, but Alice always seemed to understand him. She was patient with him and didn't focus on his social difficulties. He had a brilliant mind, and that's what she was drawn to. As she allowed herself to move past his awkwardness, she uncovered someone who was genuinely kind and funny.

"I think the last time we saw each other was when we completed our undergrad studies," she reminded him. The setting sun cast a purple hue over their faces. A warm breeze caught strands of Alice's fiery locks, lifting them from her shoulder.

Kyle thought that over and then responded, "I wanted to study engineering, and you wanted to study chemistry."

"Why didn't we stay in touch?" Alice asked. She leaned back in her chair as the waiter delivered their drinks: red wine for Alice, water with lemon for Kyle. "Thank you," she said as the glasses were placed on the white linen tablecloth covering the table.

"Are you ready to order yet?" the waiter asked.

Alice met Kyle's eyes and then replied, "No. A few more minutes?"

The waiter nodded and walked away.

"Are you sure you don't want a glass of wine or beer?" Alice asked.

Kyle shook his head. "No, I never touch the stuff."

She leaned her head back, suddenly remembering. "That's right. You never did drink alcohol in college." Lifting her glass and leaning toward Kyle, she announced, "So anyway, here's to rekindled friendships." They clinked their glasses together and then each took a sip.

"When did you start working in cryonics?" she asked, placing her glass on the table in front of her.

"I started dabbling about fifteen years ago, but only really got serious about ten years ago." Alice always had a way of putting Kyle at ease. He didn't feel like an outsider around her. He knew he could be himself, which made his usual quirkiness disappear.

"That was when you made your first breakthrough," she confirmed.

"Exactly," he said. "Had you heard about it before today?"

"Actually, I do remember reading about the first human liver transplant from donor tissue that had been removed from cryonic storage."

"We've been able to repeat the process multiple times since then, and with other organs," he said, beaming.

Alice took another sip of wine, replaced the glass on the table, and began twirling it between her fingers. "It's quite extraordinary."

He sighed heavily, staring into the glass of water in front of him. "We just haven't been able to repeat the process with a human being, only tissue."

"It's because of the brain," she remarked. "We can regenerate human tissue that's been stored via cryonics but not the human brain." She leaned in, propping her elbows on the table. "You have only frozen *dead* hosts, correct?"

"Of course," he responded.

"Once the host is pronounced dead, you only have about three minutes for the brain to make a full recovery," she stated matter-of-factly. "After cryonic storage, it's just not possible to resurrect the host and expect the brain to survive."

He shook his head and said, "I disagree."

"So then why are your test subjects failing to return to normal brain activity after cryonics?" she challenged.

He felt his palms grow moist and started rubbing them hard on his pants legs. His face was getting hot, and he began to look like a child caught in a lie.

Alice reached across the table and gently touched his arm. "Hey, I'm not trying to upset you or invalidate your work," she soothed. "I want us to figure this out together."

He looked into her emerald eyes, softened by the twilight glow. He nodded and smiled at her.

"It may be possible some day in the future," she said, leaning back in her chair, "but we're faced with a challenge today that calls for a solution. This is where I believe our projects intersect."

"Okay," he said. "I'm listening."

"Ready to order yet?" the waiter interrupted, reemerging from the shadows.

Alice looked across the table at Kyle, and he nodded. "Yes, I think we are," she said as she lifted her menu. "I'm starving."

****

"Freezing a living host isn't an option today," she resumed after their food was served. "We agree on that."

Kyle nodded as he took in a mouthful of food from his fork. The outdoor lighting had been turned on at the café, as the sky had been overtaken by darkness. They were now tented in amber lighting strung above their heads like a canopy.

"So what else can be done to suspend aging and sustain life?" she asked as she sipped her wine. "The tissue must remain alive, pumping blood and oxygen to the brain."

"But how does that accomplish the goal of suspending the aging process?"

"Good question," she said with a wink. "It doesn't. So what if, instead, we *decelerate* the aging process?"

He leaned his head back slightly and looked beyond Alice, suddenly realizing the solution had been right in front of him all along.

She returned to the food on her plate and scooped up a bite while he absorbed what she had said. The waiter approached to refill Kyle's water. Alice signaled to him that she wanted another glass of wine, and he acknowledged with a nod.

"So how do you propose we do this?" Kyle asked.

"I read that you have been experimenting with cryo-chambers in your work," she began, "but as we discussed, your tests on human hosts have failed."

Feeling full, he placed his silverware across his plate and then leaned back in his seat, taking a drink of water.

"My team has developed bio-suits that interact with the human host wearing it," she explained. "The suit was engineered to monitor physical and neurological activity by connecting to the host's bio sensory and nervous systems."

She leaned toward her companion, using her hands more as she enthusiastically described her baby: "The connections allow the suit to interact and adapt with the host's body, based on psychological and environmental stimuli, keeping the host alive."

His eyes became wide as he understood where she was going. "So what you're asking is, number one, can we use the cryo-chamber to super-cool the body without freezing it?" He held up his thumb as he spoke, then raised up his index finger as he continued, "Number two, if so, can the bio-suit keep the body and brain alive while the host is in this super-cooled state?"

She nodded, chewing a mouthful of food, as he put the puzzle together.

"And number three," he flipped up his middle finger, "can the host be warmed up in about five years and returned to normal brain activity?"

****

After dinner, Kyle and Alice were eager to test their theories. They decided to go straight to her lab and get to work. She proudly revealed the prototype of the bio-suit she had described. It was stored in a locked drawer in the lab, opened only by first entering a six-digit code on the keypad and then by scanning her hand print. Only she and her trusted assistant, Milo, had access.

"Here," she said, holding the suit in front of Kyle so he could inspect it. She held the garment as you would a fragile newborn, cradling it delicately in both hands.

"It's small," he remarked, as he examined the black material. It had the appearance of fish gills in texture and seemed luminescent in the light. He reached his hand toward the suit, drawn to it out of curiosity. As his fingers stretched closer, the fibers in the bio-suit reacted.

"What just happened?" he exclaimed, jerking his hand away.

"It's all right," she said, laughing. "Go on." She raised the garment closer to Kyle in an attempt to get him to touch it.

Once again, he raised his hand toward the bio-suit. Hovering just above it, he moved his hand from side to side and watched as the fibers reacted. The fabric was moving with him, like a wave beneath his hand. The sheen changed as if a focused beam of light was projecting from his palm, shining down onto the bio-suit.

Finally, he lowered his hand onto the fabric, on top of Alice's left hand. "It's vibrating," he exclaimed, laughing.

"It's trying to communicate with you," she explained, smiling as any proud mother would, watching her child make the first introduction to a trusted friend.

He gripped her hand, over top of the fabric, and felt the vibration increase. As he loosened his grip, the vibration subsided to a barely noticeable buzz. He slowly moved his hand across the fabric. "It's smooth," he commented, surprised at the texture.

"It's stretchable too," she said. "See?" She pulled on the garment. As the fabric stretched, the material luminesced and seemed to come alive. The vibration was audible, like a choir singing the same note as loudly as possible.

His eyes grew wide again as he felt the vibrations speed up. He watched in awe as the gill-like fibers flipped up and seemed to multiply. "This is incredible," he exclaimed, shaking his head.

"The material is biogenic," she offered. "It looks alive because it is alive."

"Biogenic," he repeated, curiously. "How did you do it?" He continued stroking the fabric as he waited for her to elaborate.

"Well, we needed a suit that would adapt quickly to any environment, including to the host," she explained. "So we started by engineering cellular textiles with similar elasticity to neoprene or spandex. Then we introduced different types of bacteria to give the textile a form of social intelligence.

"We studied how the bacteria influenced the textile's shape, color, size; this all could be manipulated by external stimuli."

"Like touch or temperature?"

"Even sound," she added. "So then we graduated to other biogenic material such as elements, secretions, and metabolites of animals, like ..."

"Fish," he remarked, observing the gill-like texture of the fabric.

"Exactly. Some fish are able to change color and shape at will, so we wanted to try and harness that ability, like we did with the bacteria. We tried a number of different specimens to get the desired effect."

"The results are incredible," he remarked, finally tearing his eyes away from the bio-suit long enough to meet Alice's gaze. "How is this even possible?"

"We had to go beyond the cellular level and manipulate the matter at the molecular level," she explained as she gently returned the bio-suit to the drawer. When she turned back around to face him, she had a black glove in her hands. It appeared to be made of the same material as the bio-suit.

"Once we had the living textile, we had to give it a brain: make it smart enough to anticipate the needs of the host wearing the suit." She handed him the glove and nodded, suggesting that he put it on. "This is when we introduced nanites."

He took the glove and noticed it felt and looked the same, but something was different. "There's no reaction from the glove, like there was from the suit."

"Slip your hand inside," she suggested.

He slowly pushed the fingers of his right hand inside the glove, stretching the material as he pulled back with his left hand. He observed the changing fibers on the outside of the glove, as he had with the bio-suit. The glove was morphing to fit his hand like a layer of skin.

"When you see the gills flip up," Alice said, "that's the nanorobotics technology allowing the textile fibers to reproduce as needed in order to expand."

What was happening inside the glove triggered an audible gasp from Kyle. He held his breath as his hand experienced a tingling sensation.

Alice placed her hand on his shoulder to calm him and to encourage him to let it happen. "The glove is attempting to communicate with you," she explained.

"It feels like my skin is crawling," he snarled, gritting his teeth as he fought the urge to rip the glove off his hand.

"It will pass in a few seconds while it's making the connection," she said reassuringly.

"Are the fibers entering my skin?"

"The nanites are, yes," she explained. "They are entering your nervous system while remaining attached to the suit. Think of the nanites as the mediator between you and the suit," she went on. "Or maybe a better example is that the nanites are the interpreter." She could feel him relax and so concluded the connection had been completed. She removed her hand from his shoulder and watched as he closed and opened his hand, getting used to his second skin.

She led him across the lab to the sink in the corner. "You, the human host, and the bio-suit are speaking different languages," she continued, "and the nanites are making it possible for you to communicate with each other."

She turned on the hot water faucet. "Using your other hand, touch the water," she said. "Careful; it's hot."

He tentatively reached forward and jerked his hand back when he felt the sting. Steam was building in the sink as the water flowed forcefully from the faucet. She took his right wrist in her hand and shoved his gloved hand into the stream of scalding water.

He started to wince, and his immediate reaction was to try and pull away, but then he calmed down and held his hand in place. She released her grip around his wrist as he continued to hold his hand under the faucet. She turned off the water.

"What did you feel?" she asked.

Kyle flexed his fingers and rolled his hand from side to side, watching steam emanate from the glove. "My brain was telling me the water was hot, but then …" He hesitated. "The glove constricted around my hand, and I felt nothing."

"It heard your warning and anticipated your needs," she explained.

"Alice, this is incredible."

****

After returning to his hotel room, Kyle went straight to work running computer simulations to modify the cryo-chambers. His brain was on fire, thinking about the bio-suit.

His lips were moving as he enthusiastically entered data into the computer, an impulse he was unaware of. His eyes were glued to the monitor, watching every character blip onto the screen, forming strings of data.

The idea of working with Alice filled him with an excitement he hadn't felt in a long time. He had been laser-focused on cryonics for so many years, since his first breakthrough. But since then, there had been little progress and even less hope.

He had felt himself losing interest in everything else as he was determined to make cryonics work, to the point that he was losing the respect of his colleagues and was more often being referred to as a "mad scientist."

Joining forces with Alice was the break he needed. He was less interested in saving human life. For him, this was more about saving himself by restoring his reputation.

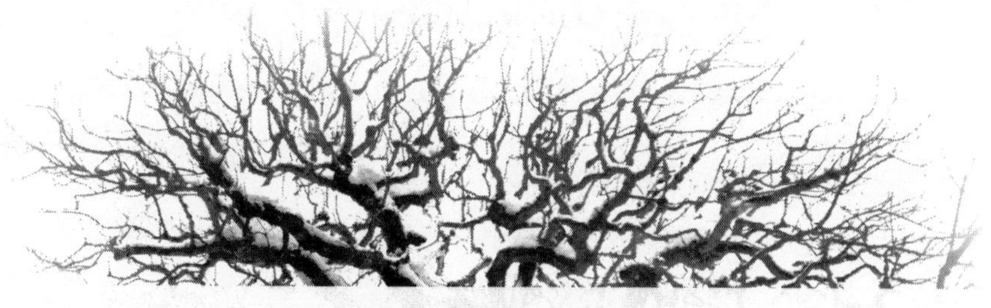

Chapter 5

"Suspended animation," Vytas repeated, skeptically, looking back and forth between Alice and Kyle.

"Yes," Alice responded excitedly.

"How is this different than cryonics?" Vytas asked, folding his arms across his chest.

"Simply put," Kyle interjected, "Cryonics would mean lowering the body temperature to the point of completely stopping all bodily functions. The host would be frozen in time."

Vytas nodded as he listened. The three of them were standing in the corner of the breakroom, huddled close for a private conversation. Alice and Kyle had arranged for this conference with Vytas before the summit resumed so they could pitch their idea.

"While I believe cryonics to be a possibility," Kyle continued, "as I mentioned yesterday, we haven't had any success to date. We are likely years away from a breakthrough—"

"And we don't have time for that," Vytas finished his thought.

"Right," Alice agreed. "So this is where suspended animation comes in. Instead of freezing the host to *stop* all bodily functions, what if we could *slow* the body?"

"You're talking about hibernation," Vytas said, looking at Alice.

"Simply put, yes. This happens in nature all the time," she added rationally. "Certain mammals will naturally enter into a hypometabolic state — coincidentally in winter — then spontaneously return to normal biological function in the spring."

"Okay," Vytas said, considering what Alice said. "Can suspended animation be artificially induced in humans?"

"Yes," Kyle answered. "It's actually been done thousands of times in cases of trauma as a way to delay the onset of cell death and provide more time for the victim to receive medical treatment."

"So you're saying it's been used as a short-term solution," Vytas said. "What you just explained is minutes or hours in a state of suspended animation." He looked back and forth from Kyle to Alice. "Am I right?"

Kyle nodded nervously. "Correct, but —"

"Has this ever been done long-term?" Vytas challenged.

"No," Alice conceded. "But we ran some simulations last night and we believe it will work."

"Okay," Vytas said. "Can you present your theory this afternoon to the rest of the Confederation?"

Alice and Kyle looked at each other as they considered the request.

"Look," Vytas stretched out his hand. "I'm not expecting visual aids and data, just a rough explanation to generate conversation. Keep it simple."

"Sure," they responded together.

"We'll be ready," Alice added.

"Great," Vytas said. Then he touched Alice on the shoulder. "I'll see you in there."

****

"For the duration of the Long Winter, we will artificially induce the host into a state of suspended animation that will slow breathing, heartbeat, and other involuntary functions to the point they are imperceptible," Kyle explained.

"If the hosts vital signs are imperceptible," a voice shouted from the audience, "is the host dead?"

"No," Alice answered. "We will be able to preserve the minimum functions in order to keep the host alive."

"How will you induce the state of suspended animation?" another voice asked.

"The cryo-chambers we are currently using for freezing biological material," Kyle responded. "They can be modified to induce this condition."

"I don't mean to be a wet blanket," Dr. Smith added, "but didn't you say yesterday that your cryonics procedures hadn't been tested on live human hosts?"

"The major flaw with cryonics is that the brain is deprived of oxygen and blood," Kyle explained. "We're not proposing that we freeze the host, but we'll get as close as we can. The host will be extremely close to death but the brain, organs, and cells will still be receiving oxygen and blood."

"Keeping the brain alive and stimulated," Alice added, "will allow us to fully restore the host to normal mental, physical and biological function at the end of the Long Winter, essentially bringing the host out of hibernation."

"Is this even possible?" a voice from the audience shouted over the other murmurs.

"Yes, suspended animation is widely used in the medical field today," Alice answered. "Dr. Wong, I'm sure you've heard of the procedure," she added, gesturing toward the leader of group twelve in the audience.

Dr. Wong stood in front of his chair and responded, "Yes, I've used this procedure during heart surgery," he added, trying to speak loudly. "The brain will still be receiving oxygen and blood, but," he paused as he noticed one of the assistants jogging toward him with a microphone. He switched it on and then repeated, "I have used suspended animation during heart surgery, but only to *temporarily* preserve life during a procedure. What you're suggesting has never been done."

"That is correct," Alice conceded.

Someone else in the audience stood and said, in a soft voice, "I have a question." She paused while an assistant brought a microphone. "You said that you would keep the brain alive and stimulated; what do you mean by that?"

"Great question," Alice responded. "My team has developed highly sophisticated bio-suits, engineered to monitor physical and neurological activity by connecting to the hosts' bio sensory and nervous systems.

"These connections allow the suit to interact and adapt with the host's body based on psychological and environmental stimuli, and to keep the host alive."

The woman who asked the question was still standing while Alice responded. "You're saying the suit is meant to adapt based on external stimuli?" she asked, puzzled. "Will there be external stimuli if the host is hibernating?"

"So the original intention behind the suit's design was for living, active hosts," Alice explained. "We were looking for options based on space exploration, deep sea, or Eastern Hemisphere missions where the host would need the suit to adapt to the environment.

"But we believe the suit can be modified to provide the stimulation to a host that is immobilized, such as during suspended animation."

"What sort of stimulation, and for what purpose?" the woman asked. Then she took her seat while Alice explained.

"While the host is in stasis for a length of time—let's say five years—the body will suffer. There will be significant atrophy of the body tissues and organs. The host will not be drinking or eating, so there will also be dramatic weight loss.

"Neurologically, the brain will be alive but without the host working, learning, creating, or communicating, it's not clear how the brain will be affected by this on a long-term basis.

"It's our belief," Alice motioned to Kyle, indicating she was speaking for him as well, "that the bio-suit can be re-engineered to provide everything the body needs, physically and mentally, during the Long Winter while the host is in suspended animation.

"The suit will integrate with the host's central nervous system to artificially mimic bodily functions, such as awareness, movements, sensations, thoughts, speech, and memory. Think of this as exercising the brain.

"The suit will also link with the host's cardiovascular and muscular systems to stimulate and maintain muscle tone and to circulate blood, oxygen, and carbon dioxide throughout the body," Alice added. "This will ensure that when the hosts emerge from hibernation, they only feel rested."

The audience was awash in muffled chatter while Kyle and Alice remained at the podium on stage. They waited for additional questions but they did not come. Vytas emerged from their right and made his way to them. His microphone was still fixed to this shirt collar, but it was off. Enough of his voice was audible on the podium microphone to hear him thank Kyle and Alice, and then he motioned for them to exit the stage.

Vytas turned to face the audience. He started to speak but then remembered his microphone was off. He clicked the button then repeated,

"Everyone, let's thank Dr. Weber and Dr. Wallace for their impromptu briefing."

The audience applauded, starting with about half of the group first before spreading throughout the room. It lasted for about ten seconds and then fizzled out, and discussions started again.

Vytas attempted to quiet the room, subtly at first by motioning with his hands. This was unsuccessful, so he decided to be more direct. "Quiet down, please," he said, waiting for the noise to fade.

"Let's take the rest of the day to digest what we've learned over the last several days," he suggested. "Use this time to speak with each other privately, brainstorm at your own pace.

"Tomorrow is the last day of the summit," he continued. "My assistants have been taking copious notes of our debate. Based on what's been discussed, they will draft a proposal for our review tomorrow.

"I do not anticipate we will have the final product before our summit concludes," he conceded, "so we will all need to remain engaged after we leave here tomorrow. We all have jobs to return to, but finalizing this resolution needs to remain our focus and our priority."

Vytas looked around, confirming he had everyone's attention and that there were no questions. "See you all back here tomorrow."

****

Vytas pressed his lips gently to Hanita's neck as he slowly stroked the curve of her side, up along her hip and around to her thigh then back up again. They lay in silence, naked bodies pressed together in his bed, savoring the moment. He gently caressed the back of her salty shoulder with his lips then propped his head up in his hand.

"What are you thinking?" he asked.

She turned her body to face him and his arm naturally draped around her. "That I wish we had met before we found out the world was ending."

"I know you're scared but we have ten years before the Long Winter," he reminded her.

"I am scared," she agreed. "And angry; it's a lot to take in."

He listened as he studied her body, searching for hidden constellations amongst the freckles and beauty marks. This had become his new, favorite hobby over the last week as they grew closer.

"What will happen after the Long Winter?" she asked. "What will happen to us?"

His fingers found their way down her side, up the curve of her hip and around before resting on the outside of her waist. "I thought you believed in fate," he reminded her.

He pulled her closer to his body and raised his lips to her ear. His voice tingled as he began, "Long ago, King Cepheus and his Queen Cassiopeia reigned in a faraway land. And they had a daughter named Andromeda."

She rolled onto her back and moaned, "I love this story, V." The corners of her lips turned up in a sultry smile.

"The queen," he continued, "proclaimed Andromeda to be even more beautiful than the nymphs of the sea. But this angered the nymphs. Full of jealousy and spite, the nymphs cried to Neptune for retribution and in response, he unleashed the sea monster Cetus to wreak vengeance upon the boastful queen."

She was captivated as he began to recite the mythical story with enthusiasm and passion, like a love poem. She laid her hand atop his and they laced their fingers together.

"Cetus ravaged the shores of the kingdom," he growled, "with his sharp teeth." She squealed with delight as he playfully bit her neck. She quickly rolled to face him again, wrapping tightly around his body. He stroked the small of her back as they melted into each other's eyes.

"Desperate, King Cepheus offered Andromeda as a sacrifice, advised this was the only way to stop the monster's rampage and save the city." He rolled atop her and took hold of her wrists, pinning her to the bed. "Andromeda was chained to a rock and left for Cetus to devour.

"Just as the monster charged at the young princess, the hero Perseus, having heard Andromeda's cries, appeared in the sky."

"Help, help," she giggled, writhing beneath him.

He rose up on his knees, straddling her body, his eyes fixed on hers. With excitement he continued, "Mounted on the great winged horse Pegasus, Perseus swooped between the monster and its prey.

"Perseus pulled Medusa's severed head from his satchel." Raising his arm, fist clenched, he hissed, "a head so hideous that all who looked upon it were instantly turned to stone.

"The monster was no exception. Cetus gazed into Medusa's eyes and froze, defeated, before he sunk to the bottom of the sea."

He flopped beside Hanita, and she rolled to face him. His voice much softer now, he cradled her face in his hand and said, "Perseus immediately fell in love with the beautiful Andromeda. And he carried her off to be his bride.

"The figures of the Andromeda story were placed in the sky, and right here," his eyes moved to her abdomen and his fingers traced a shape formed by her freckles. Then he looked up into her eyes.

"The story of Andromeda and Perseus is a love story with a tragic beginning," he said softly. "Not unlike the beginning of our story."

Sounding more serious now, he continued, "We can't change how or what brought us together. But we found each other.

"I don't know what will happen tomorrow, or in ten years, or after the Long Winter," he confessed, as he gently wiped a tear from her cheek. "But we have now."

They made love again before exhaustion consumed them, and they fell asleep.

Chapter 6

The small press briefing room was packed full of reporters and photographers. Monitors were set up at each side of the small stage, facing the audience, and a podium was in the center. An announcement was planned to be broadcast live for all of the United Western Territories.

The room was loud as the invitees filed in and visited with each other. The briefing by the Confederation spokesperson was scheduled to begin at eighteen hundred hours, and there was much speculation about what would be announced.

A door at the left side of the stage opened, and a tall, thin woman walked through. She was wearing navy blue slacks and a matching suit jacket. Her jacket was open, revealing a delicate pink, conservative blouse, buttoned to the neck. Her golden hair flowed just past her jawline in thick waves.

She walked up to the podium and pulled a pair of glasses from the inside jacket pocket as she laid the portfolio she was carrying down in front of her. The glasses were burgundy in color and the rectangular shape complimented her long features.

Seeing that the briefing was about to start, the audience members quickly quieted down and found their assigned seats. They readied their recording devices and then waited. At exactly eighteen hundred hours, a person in front of the speaker counted down from five and then pointed at her, indicating she was live.

"Good evening," she began. "My name is Dr. Ariel Goldwyn, press secretary and spokesperson for the Confederation of the United Western Territories.

"What I'm about to tell you is highly technical and frightening, so I'm going to speak slowly and keep this at a very basic level." Dr. Goldwyn paused and looked around the room, making eye contact with the members of the press before adding, "Please hold all of your questions until the end of the briefing."

Looking back into the large video camera positioned in front of her and broadcasting her speech, she continued, "For those of you watching the live stream, there will be much more detailed information distributed after the briefing so that everyone may read about and understand exactly what I am about to discuss. We will also make staff available to answer your questions for as long as necessary."

Dr. Goldwyn stood tall as she spoke, occasionally looking down at her prepared speech and around the room but mostly keeping her eyes focused on the video camera. She needed the viewing audience to trust her, so she wanted to appear confident and strong.

"Six months ago, the Confederation held a special, week-long summit." The two monitors behind her on her left and right sides suddenly came to life. "Representatives from the astronomy and physics departments learned that a large cloud of space dust, containing meteors and harmful chemicals, is moving toward our planet."

A computerized rendition appeared on the monitors, depicting the cloud of space dust, in motion.

"It's difficult to tell by the animation," she admitted, pointing at the monitor on her right, "but the cloud is still tens of millions of miles away.

"At the same time, this team also detected that our planet had been gradually shifting off of its axis, and our rotation is slowing." Dr. Goldwyn's hands remained on the podium except when she flipped the pages in front of her.

The animation on the monitors changed to depict side-by-side images of the planet at its normal axial tilt and rotation, and where the scientists estimate it will eventually end up.

"These events are caused by the Jupiter explosion that occurred one hundred years ago. The particles and meteors in the space cloud are bits of Jupiter and its moons. And without Jupiter in orbit, our planet is unable to maintain proper rotation and unable to remain properly on its axis."

Dr. Goldwyn paused while there were audible gasps in the room. The reporters were looking side to side at each other, murmuring and chattering. She lifted a glass of water from below the podium and took a small sip. Pens moved quickly across pages. Fingers tapped feverishly on tiny keypads. Cameras clicked and clacked loudly in front of her. She placed the glass back in its place then cleared her throat.

"Each of these events would be considered potentially extinction level in their own right," she continued, quieting the room. "What our team learned is that these events will peak at the same time in a little less than ten years from now, and the result will be another ice age, lasting at least five years."

Dr. Goldwyn then added, "The Confederation is referring to this period as the Long Winter."

The reporters stirred restlessly in their seats, waiting impatiently to ask questions. Dr. Goldwyn remained steadfast in her deliverance of the prepared speech but also allowed time for the reporters to react to her words before moving on.

"The good news is that the ice age will end," she said reassuringly. "Our experts believe that the planet's proper rotation and axis will be restored after the cloud of space dust passes by.

"The Confederation convened to discuss these three urgent crises and to form a plan for our survival." Dr. Goldwyn had reached the part of her speech that she dreaded. She became noticeably uncomfortable. Her eyes lingered on the page in front of her too long, and she shifted her weight from left to right.

"This is where it becomes complicated," she announced, finally looking up and into the camera again.

"It's not possible to survive the Long Winter on the surface. Our planet will essentially go into hibernation as the ground freezes, depleting our resources. We have determined our best chance for survival is for us to hibernate as well.

"Together, we will construct massive underground sites, known as Cradles, and we will wait out the Long Winter at these sites in hibernation." Dr. Goldwyn paused, straightening her back as she breathed deeply, mustering the strength to go on.

“The Confederation has had to make some difficult, painful decisions regarding who is suitable for hibernation,” she said, stoically.

“If you are sick or over a certain age, you may not be eligible for hibernation.” She added empathetically, “There is also a danger that the process will have damaging effects if you are *under* a certain age.”

“For this reason,” she took a pause before continuing, “we will not accept anyone younger than nine years of age for hibernation.”

The room became silent except for the click, click, click of cameras. The reporters had sucked all the oxygen out of the room after Dr. Goldwyn delivered the startling news. It took a few seconds for the words to sink in, and then they began murmuring, writing, and typing again.

“I know this sounds cruel,” Dr. Goldwyn admitted, “but we set this age limit to allow time for current pregnancies to continue to delivery and to also give couples time to decide how they want to move forward with family planning.

“As free citizens, you may opt out of hibernation.” Dr. Goldwyn shrugged her shoulders as she added, “This is your choice and your right. We will require some staff at each site to keep watch over the hibernation chambers, and we will make available some space in the Cradles for this purpose.

“This will not be an option for everyone, and it will not be an easy life,” she rationalized, pursing her lips. “You will be alone, and you will be underground for the duration of the Long Winter. Food will be rationed.”

Dr. Goldwyn cleared her throat and then steadily delivered her final words: “For the next ten years, we must all work together in order for this plan to be successful. We will all have jobs directly or indirectly related to this plan. Unrest will not be tolerated. Lawbreaking will still be investigated and prosecuted.

“My fellow citizens, know this,” she said proudly. “History will judge us on what we do next. We can give in and do nothing; that would be easy. Or we can work together and hopefully, in twenty years, we will still be around to be judged.

“Now, I will take a few questions.” She reached for her glass of water as reporters began calling out questions. She pointed to one reporter directly in front of her as she replaced the glass.

"Thank you, doctor," the report said as he stood up. "You mentioned our resources will be depleted when the planet freezes…how will we survive once the Long Winter is over?"

"That's a great question," Dr. Goldwyn responded. "This will be accomplished in several ways. First, we plan to start stockpiling seeds and grains immediately. We will be asking farmers and meat processing plants to ramp up production in the short-term so that we may create a cache of dried protein.

"We will also be developing dehydrated meals so that once out of hibernation," she explained, "we will have food ready to eat that is easy to distribute.

"At some point in the future," she continued, "we will be asking our farmers to begin scaling down. This includes at our livestock farms as well as fruit and vegetables, all of it.

"Finally, we have a team looking into how we may restart the food supply chain once the Long Winter is over." She paused before adding, "I am not able to provide a lot of detail here but I can say this involves using cryonics to store animal embryos."

The reporter looked confused. "How..." He struggled to form the question he wanted to ask.

"More detail around this will be provided at a later date," she responded, cutting him off. Then she pointed at another person.

"Dr. Goldwyn," the reporter said, standing in front of her seat. "How many Cradle sites will there be?"

"We are still finalizing the number and locations for the Cradles," she replied. "To date, ten sites have been selected."

The image on the monitors changed to depict where the ten selected sites were located in the Western Hemisphere.

"The information packet that will be distributed at the end of the briefing and online," she added, "will provide the exact locations of these sites."

Hands shot up again, but the first reporter was still standing; she asked, "When will the number of sites be finalized?"

"We have a list of other potential sites that are being considered, but the final number will depend on the response from the citizens," Dr. Goldwyn stated. "We are asking for each citizen to notify the Confederation of their choice so we may plan accordingly."

Dr. Goldwyn then pointed at another reporter.

He jumped up from his seat and asked, "Is there a deadline for citizens to respond, and will they be allowed to change their mind?"

"Yes," Dr. Goldwyn replied, "there is a deadline to respond." She glanced to her right at one of her staffers who held up a notepad with words scribbled on it so she could read it. "The deadline is one year from today.

"As for changing your decision," she continued, "once the deadline has passed, that is not an option."

Another hand rose up from the middle of the crowd. "Yes," Dr. Goldwyn said, pointing at the new speaker.

The reporter stood in front of her seat and asked, "When will you begin digging at the selected sites?"

"Well, for the ten sites we've already selected," Dr. Goldwyn responded with a heavy sigh, "we have already begun planning. Teams of excavators and demolition experts will be assembled at each site."

As she was speaking, Dr. Goldwyn was flipping through the pages in front of her, stalling until she found what she was looking for. "The plan is to break ground in about six months, but we are still looking for a project coordinator."

Chapter 7

Vytas's eyes shifted upward from the monitor, briefly diverting his attention away from the colleague he was speaking with over video chat. Kyle was pacing nervously outside his office. Vytas motioned for him to come in and have a seat.

Kyle entered the office and sat across from Vytas at his desk. He looked around, trying not to listen to the conversation happening in front of him. His eyes moved over the papers on the desk, lingering too long on the document on top.

"Let me get back to you," Vytas said, watching Kyle as he laid a folder over the document. "What can I do for you, Kyle?" he asked after he ended the chat.

Kyle quickly refocused his attention from the document back to Vytas. He took a deep breathe in and asked, "Do you know what rare metals are?"

Vytas sighed heavily and said, "Yes, of course."

"There are seventeen chemical elements in the periodic table known as rare metals," Kyle explained with excitement. "The first rare mineral was discovered in 1787—"

Vytas loudly cleared his throat, interrupting. "Get to the point, Kyle."

"Sorry," Kyle apologized. "Rare elements like dysprosium, neodymium, and terbium are used to make things like lithium-ion batteries, electric motors, solar panels ..."

"Can you get to the point, please?" Vytas urged, rubbing his forehead impatiently.

"We need these elements, but we don't have enough of them," Kyle blurted out.

Vytas waited for Kyle to continue, but the previously impatient scientist remained silent. Vytas raised his eyebrows and stretched out his palm, inviting Kyle to add more. "Can we get them?"

"Not in the Western Hemisphere." Kyle leaned toward Vytas and rested his forearms on the desk. "But I think there's a way to get them in the Eastern Hemisphere."

Vytas shook his head and said, "No way."

"Hear me out," Kyle begged.

"The Eastern Hemisphere is not safe, Kyle. You know that."

"We need these metals, and others, or you can forget surviving the Long Winter," Kyle exclaimed, his hands balled into fists.

Vytas leaned back in his chair, eyes locked on Kyle's. He looked away for a moment while he thought about how to respond to this outburst. "Do you know what that conversation was about that you interrupted?" he asked, motioning toward the monitor on his desk.

Kyle swallowed hard as he unclenched his fists. "No."

"There was an accident at one of the dig sites. People were hurt, maybe killed. They are still trying to confirm everyone's whereabouts."

Kyle could feel the heat building in his neck and spreading up to his cheeks. He began blinking uncontrollably. "I'm sorry, I —"

Vytas sprang forward in his chair, looking directly at Kyle. "I'm not finished." He paused and looked down at his desk. "Today of all days," he said softly to himself, shaking his head slowly from side to side.

"A year ago, when I was asked to be project lead over construction of the Cradle sites, I didn't want to accept. I knew it would be a burden." He lifted his head and met Kyle's apologetic eyes. "I knew there would be days like this."

He lowered his eyes to the folder on his desk, placed strategically to conceal what was underneath. He touched his fingers to the folder, sliding the folder forward and backward, not enough to disclose what was hidden. The rhythmic motion was calming and gave Vytas time to think.

"I know it's hard for you to communicate, Kyle," he continued, still watching the folder slide from side to side. "I know you don't always understand what others are feeling, and you don't always know what to say or how to say it." Vytas leaned back in his chair again and folded his arms across his chest. "I'm going to cut you some slack out of respect for Alice, but I need you to focus."

He sighed heavily and asked, "Why is mining rare metals in the Eastern Hemisphere important to our survival?"

Kyle took a moment to gather his thoughts, considering what Vytas had said and what he was asking of him. Then he finally answered, "The falling temperatures leading up to and during the Long Winter will cause the power grid to fail. We're going to need an alternate power source. In order to build it, we will need rare metals."

Vytas thought for a moment. "I'm not saying yes, but leave me your proposal by tomorrow morning, and I'll read it over."

Kyle forced a smile on his face and then quickly pushed up from the chair and headed toward the door. He paused before walking out and turned to look back at Vytas. "Congratulations," he said.

Vytas had returned to the monitor in front of him but then looked up at Kyle, wondering what he meant.

Kyle motioned at the document hiding under the folder. "I … couldn't help but read it," he explained.

Vytas's eyes shifted to the desk and then back up to Kyle. "Thanks," he replied, then watched as Kyle walked away.

Vytas's eyes returned to the folder. As he slid it aside, he could hear the familiar "clack, clack, clack" coming from the hallway, growing louder and louder until it stopped, just outside of his office.

Vytas's eyes lifted from the desk to see the white, three-inch heels Hanita was wearing today instead of the traditional black. As he continued looking up, his eyes caressed the white dress that had replaced her normal security uniform. The hem flowed demurely just below her knees. The dress fit snuggly on her body, accentuating all of her curves. Her wavy brunette locks were down today, cascading just over her bare shoulders.

"Ready, V?" she asked. She gracefully pulled her hair to one side as she sashayed into his office, hips rolling from side to side.

Vytas lifted the Application for Marriage License from his desk and slid it into the folder. The he stood up and moved toward her. "Almost," he said, smiling.

She closed the top button of his crisp, white shirt. He lifted his chin while she gently tightened up and straightened the Windsor knot on his cobalt-colored tie. This was the first time she had seen him wear a tie and thought to herself what a shame it was that he did not wear one more often.

"There," she said as she admired her work, sliding her hands across his chest. She met his eyes and asked, "Where's your suit jacket?"

"Behind the door," he answered, tucking his shirt into his black slacks and then tugging at the cuffs on his shirt sleeves.

She turned to retrieve his jacket. She pulled the door away from the wall and carefully lifted the black suit jacket from the hanger. When she turned back, she gasped as she noticed he was holding a small bouquet of petite, short-stemmed burgundy roses, encircled by a blue sash to match his tie.

"Alice said you weren't going to carry a bouquet, but I thought you might want to."

"They're beautiful," she crooned. She returned to him and took the flowers while passing him the suit jacket. She buried her nose into the blossoms, inhaling the sweet aroma.

"Alice is meeting us there," he said as he took her hand and led her to the doorway. She rested her head on his shoulder, feeling very lucky as they left the building and made their way to the courthouse.

****

Kyle's proposal to mine for rare metals in the amber zone of the Eastern Hemisphere had been approved, with the strict orders to not enter the red zone. He had spent the last six months making the necessary preparations, starting by pulling up the latest satellite imagery and precisely mapping out the amber zone.

Then he divided this three-million-square-mile area into acre-sized plots. He now had the overwhelming task of meticulously examining approximately 1.9 million separate grids, a task that could take more than a year.

He had loaded up an aircraft with the gear he would need to locate, mine, collect, and transport the rare metals, all without leaving the lab.

Kyle would fly the aircraft into the amber zone using remote controls, radar, and cameras installed on the aircraft. He had equipped the aircraft with ground-penetrating radar that would be able to detect the rare metals under the surface.

Once a cache was located, Kyle would land the aircraft and dispatch a mining robot from onboard. He had designed and built the robot himself. He was so proud of his creation that he even affixed his name on it, just in case anyone wondered who it belonged to.

The autonomous mining robot would create a tunnel using explosives to break apart the rocks, extract the minerals from the mine shaft, carry the samples back to the aircraft, and store them securely for transport back to the lab.

Today, Kyle would begin his virtual expedition. The excitement swelled inside him. He would find the rare metals and build the critical power sources needed for their survival. He would save everyone.

Failure was not an option.

****

"How's it going?" Alice asked, looking over Kyle's shoulder at the screen in front of them.

"Slow," he replied, unenthusiastically.

"How long have you been at it?"

He sat up straight to stretch his back. "Two weeks, three days," he replied, looking at the time in the lower right corner of the monitor in front of him. "Four hours, six minutes," he groaned. "And not a single hit."

"Don't lose hope." She gave his shoulder a squeeze of encouragement. "See you for dinner tonight?"

"Looking forward to it," he replied, smiling up at her.

"Eight o'clock," she confirmed.

He nodded his head and grunted his agreement without looking away from the monitor.

"Okay. I'll leave you to it, then." She removed her hand from his shoulder and then stood to walk out. "See you later."

****

Kyle almost didn't notice the flashing orange box in the lower right corner of the screen. He had been staring at this monitor every day, eighteen hours a day, for the last four months. For most people, this would strain their mental health, being isolated in a lab, without social interaction, only watching digital images on a small screen. But for Kyle, that was the easy part.

What was eating at Kyle was that he had yet to find any rare minerals, and he was already about a quarter of the way through the expedition.

He stopped typing and touched the flashing box on the screen with his right index finger. A chat window appeared on the monitor:

Alice: *You're working late.*

A part of Kyle missed Alice, but another part of him thought of her as a distraction. He rationalized that communication is what she needed. He could multitask while speaking with her and not lose any time on his project.

Kyle: *Still working meticulously through my grid search. What's your excuse?*

Alice: *I'm working too.*

Kyle: *This is taking a lot more time than I thought. Sorry I haven't been as available lately.*

Alice: *I understand. Am I interrupting?*

He wanted to say, "Yes. Now let me get back to work." But he knew how hurtful that would be. Ever since his outburst with Vytas he thought about what Vytas said; Kyle knew he had to try harder.

Before starting this expedition, he and Alice had been spending more time together, getting closer. He didn't want to jeopardize what their relationship was becoming. *What* was *it becoming*? he wondered. He was learning from her how to interact socially, though it did not come naturally to him. It was forced, but he appeared to be getting better at it.

Kyle: *Never.*

Alice: *Want some company? I could come in, since I'm working anyway.*

Kyle bit his lip, eager to return to his work. He wanted to end the chat but was aware that he needed to do it in a respectful way. In his mind, this was progress. He was showing empathy, albeit forced.

Kyle: *I won't be very good company tonight. Maybe another time?*

Alice: *No worries. I'll let you get back to work.*

****

Alice was quiet, pushing the food around on her plate.

"Not hungry?" Hanita asked. She looked forward to the once-a-week lunch she and Alice had, but today, her friend was distant.

"It's Kyle," she replied. "He's been at this mining expedition for nine months now, and we rarely see each other anymore." She laid her fork across her plate. "I'm worried about him."

"You know how he is," Hanita replied. "Once he's found what he's looking for." She paused, considering her next words carefully.

"Once he's found what he's looking for," Alice repeated. "What?"

"Well," she continued, "I was going to say that he will return to normal. But then I remembered, normal for Kyle isn't that much better than what he is now."

They both laughed. Having lunch with Hanita was exactly what Alice needed to make her feel better. She needed to laugh at the situation she had put herself in and move on.

"Oh, what was I thinking?" she asked out loud as her giggling subsided with a musical sigh.

Hanita wanted to offer an opinion. Instead, she returned to the half-eaten lunch on her plate and scooped up a mouthful of food to prevent her thoughts from being verbalized. That wouldn't be good for their friendship. And now that they were in-laws, she couldn't risk it.

"I really like Kyle," Alice admitted. "I felt like we were finally making a connection, like a relationship with him was possible."

Hanita nodded as she ate, letting Alice do all the talking.

"I thought it would be romantic to spend the Long Winter with Kyle, awake in the Cradle," she continued, as her mind drifted far away.

"I imagined what it would be like, just the two of us." A seductive smile formed on her lips as she stared at her plate and twirled her fork.

"What are you thinking now?" Hanita asked.

"That it will be a long winter in more ways than one," Alice bemoaned.

"What will you do?"

"What can I do?" Alice replied as she took in a bite from her fork. "The deadline has passed." After a moment, she swallowed and then took a sip of water. "It will be fine. It makes sense for me and Kyle to remain awake during the Long Winter. The chambers and the bio-suits are our designs, so if anything goes wrong, we should be awake."

"You're right," Hanita agreed.

"I'm just worried that he's too unstable to handle it."

****

Kyle was nearing the conclusion of the amber zone expedition, one year, three weeks, and four days from when he started. He watched the monitor as the aircraft moved over the last of the 1.9 million grids. He had been working almost around the clock and was sleeping in short intervals at the lab. He hadn't showered in weeks and had been existing on coffee and one meal a day.

He had been avoiding everyone lately, especially Alice. She should be the one he leaned on, but he didn't want her to see him like this. Most of all, he didn't want her pity; he wanted her respect. The only way he could earn her respect was for this mining expedition to succeed.

But he was running out of time. That was why he had been avoiding Alice. It was becoming increasingly difficult to tell her that he hadn't found anything. So the last time they had spoken, feeling quite confident, he had lied to her. He was so certain that he would have found the rare metals by now, so what was the harm in a white lie?

But now, the thought of having to confess he had lied was unbearable. He winced at the pain in his gut, manifested by his own failure and deceit.

An idea had taken root in his mind. He had brushed it off, but now the idea was growing, feeding off of his weakness, shame, and need for success.

If he explored the forbidden red zone, would anyone know?

****

Alice was startled by the loud bang of the door slamming open. She quickly spun her chair around to see Kyle rushing into the room, dodging desks, lab techs, and stray chairs. She barely recognized him. He appeared unkempt, thinner, but happy.

She hadn't spoken to Kyle in over a month, since he told her he had detected a trace signature of the rare metals he was searching for. She had expected him to announce success much sooner after that, but instead, he had retreated from her. Alice assumed this meant it was a false reading, and he didn't want to admit it.

"Alice," he panted, "I found it."

"Oh?" her response was interrupted when Kyle gripped her shoulders tight and kissed her directly on the lips.

"See you for dinner tonight?" he asked.

She had lost the ability to speak. The kiss was unexpected and new. Her eyes were big, her mouth agape, and the only response she was able to give was to mirror his excitement and nod.

"Eight o'clock," Kyle exclaimed as he backed away. Then he quickly turned and ran toward the door, stumbling over a chair leg on the way.

Alice glanced over at Hanita, perched at her standup desk, and shrugged her shoulders. Then she returned to the monitor in front of her and continued with her work. She was smiling now, comforted at the thought of the old Kyle returning.

****

"Kyle," Alice said softly. He was slumped over his workstation, asleep. She grasped his shoulder and shook him gently. "Kyle, wake up."

"Huh?" Kyle began to stir and lift his head up. He turned his head left and right, and stretched his arms across the desk. "What time is it?"

"It's early," she responded. "You must have slept here all night." He hadn't pulled an all-nighter since he located the cache of rare metals six months ago, the day he burst into her lab, full of excitement and hope. Now, she was worried that he might be pulling away from her again, retreating into his work.

He rubbed his eyes and sat up straight. His fingers dug in deeper as he remembered what happened the night before. He couldn't look at Alice, so he touched a key on the keyboard in front of him, and the monitor came to life.

"Are you on the way to your lab?" he asked as he started typing.

She had the old Kyle back for a short time, since the day he discovered the large deposit of rare metals. Now she realized he had been replaced again by the sullen, hollow version of Kyle.

"Yes," she said, sighing. "I just wanted to check in on you."

"I'm going to be pretty busy here today," he remarked.

"You brought the expedition aircraft back last night, right?"

He swallowed hard and continued typing. "How did you —"

"Everyone's talking about it."

He turned around. "Everyone's talking about what?" He was shaking now. His curly black hair was wet with sweat and glued to his forehead.

"It's pretty exciting stuff, Kyle." She tried to soothe him with her tone. "That's all I meant."

He lowered his eyes and turned back to the monitor. "I'm sorry for snapping. I haven't gotten a lot of sleep lately," he admitted.

"I'll let you get back to work," she said. Then she turned and walked out.

He waited a few seconds before looking over his shoulder to confirm he was alone. Then he opened the bottom drawer of the desk and stealthily removed the half-full bottle of whiskey from inside. He unscrewed the lid and gulped directly from the bottle, wincing as he swallowed. He wanted to forget last night.

****

Hanita heard the rush of water coming from the master bathroom and knew Vytas was awake. She folded closed the cover of the photo album, saving the page with her fingers, and then lifted it from the coffee table. She carried it and her mug of tea out of the living room and down the hallway.

As she approached the office on the right side of the hallway, she noticed the door had managed to swing open again. She squeezed the book against her chest and quickly pulled the door closed before moving on, taking care not to look inside. She rarely looked inside.

Now inside the master bedroom, she walked toward the window, opposite the bathroom. She gently laid the photo album onto the dresser, bathed in the light coming from the window directly above it, and opened it to the saved page.

The squeak from the bathroom faucet signaled that Vytas was finished. She sipped from the mug with her back facing the master bathroom and she imagined him there in the doorway: the soft rustling of the white t-shirt as he folded his arms across his chest; the subtle creak as he leaned against the door frame; the sound of his heart beating.

"You're not fooling anyone," she teased, singing. Her right elbow was on her hip, and she was holding the mug of tea out to her side.

"Am I that obvious?" he asked, surrendering to her.

Brunette locks streaked with the colors of a Tuscan sunset spilled over her soft shoulders. She was draped in a knee-length black robe, patterned with white lilies. Her naked legs extended from the hem of the robe, tantalizing and firm.

"Perhaps I'm just that good." She playfully wiggled her hips as she taunted him. It was difficult to sneak up on a senior security officer.

"So what has you so captivated over there, Nita?" Still in the doorway, he craned his neck, trying to see around her.

"You," she swooned. She lifted the back of the book off the desk so he could see it was their photo album she was flipping through.

"Do you remember the day we met?" she asked.

He closed his eyes and sighed, saying, "It was seven years ago, on a Monday. The first day of the summit. The day I fell in love." He let the memory cascade over him and wrap him in a warm embrace.

"I remember how you sauntered up to me, so confident." She stroked the page in front of her as she remembered the rush of their first introduction.

Vytas pushed away from the door frame and began to slowly make his way toward his wife. "I was terrified," he admitted, eyes open but far away.

She spun around. Their eyes met, and she could see him smiling. "You were not," she challenged.

He simply nodded. "But I knew I would have only one opportunity to impress you." He reached for her hand and dove into her dark, smoldering eyes.

"So I told myself I would make it count." He leaned his head back and wondered aloud, "Do you remember what I said to you?"

She brought the back of her other hand to her forehead, as if swooning, and gasped dramatically. "I won't ever forget it."

She climbed into his arms, kissing him hard on the lips. She slipped her hands beneath his t-shirt; his warm skin seemed to come alive as her fingers brushed across his chest, sexy tufts of hair creeping down his abdomen, disappearing below the waistband of his boxer shorts. He tightened his grip on her hips as he pulled her close.

Their bodies reacted with shockwaves rippling through every cell as their lips touched. Their kiss was deep and wet. She gently took his lip between her teeth. They enjoyed using every part of their bodies to make love, igniting all of their senses.

She felt herself losing touch with reality as passion took over. She pushed his t-shirt up, and he pulled it over his head, throwing it to the floor. She slid her tongue slowly up his neckline until she reached his ear.

"I'm yours, always," she purred. Then she slowly moved down his body, sliding his boxers off.

He easily lifted her into his arms, and they pressed their lips together. She wrapped her thighs tightly around his waist and combed her fingers through his hair.

"You're not wearing anything under your robe," he said, breathing hard.

He moved his hand up her back to the collar of the robe she was wearing and gently pulled it down. She lowered her arms, allowing the robe to fall to her waist. Then she untied the sash, and the robe landed in a pile on the floor beneath them.

He paused to admire her naked body, caressing her with his eyes. He allowed her to lean back in his arms, and her thighs squeezed tighter against his body as he took her breast in his mouth. She gasped as his teeth tugged at her nipple, gripping his shoulders forcefully in approval. Anticipation was building in them both.

He brought her to the bed and gently laid her down, still between her thighs. She could feel his lips on her skin as he continued down her body. His breathe was warm, his tongue, wet, his hands, gentle. She stretched her arms above her head.

He moved his mouth past her belly button, stroking her outer thighs with his hands. As he moved lower, he slipped his hands under her body, lifting and parting her legs. She watched as he licked one of her inner thighs and then the other before pulling her closer and taking her in his mouth.

She moaned sweetly as he used his tongue. The sensation building within her was thrilling, exciting; she was floating. She entwined her fingers in his hair and pulled him deeper. She began to breathe faster and bit her lip as her legs began to quiver on his shoulders. After a moment, she became calm.

He prowled his way back up her body, nibbling at her skin as he moved, until he was looking into her satiated eyes. She tasted his still wet lips and then moaned softly as he pushed himself inside her.

He moved in and out, her hips pushing rhythmically toward him with each thrust and pulling away in time with his movement, in and out.

Kissing, touching, and licking, back and forth.

Grasping, pulling, biting, pulsing.

With one arm around her back and the other grabbing her buttocks, he rose to his knees while pulling her close in one fluid move. She wrapped her legs tightly around his waist. He balanced her on his thighs as he continued moving in and out.

Thrusting, sweating, arching … faster.

Until finally, gasping and moaning, they tumbled as one onto the bed, out of breath, sweaty and satisfied. They lay quietly, arms gently folded around each other, as their breathing slowed. She snuggled closer to him, craving the warmth of his body.

"Are you cold?" he asked.

"A little," she whispered, feeling exhausted.

He snatched the blanket from the foot of the bed and pulled it over their bodies. "Did I mention, I'm doing a walk-through of the lab next week."

"No," she sighed. "Why?"

"I'm the project leader," he said, chuckling. "It's my job."

"Obviously," she giggled, playfully tickling his side. "I mean, is there any particular reason?"

"In two more years, we will start the hibernation," he answered. "I want to make sure we're on schedule."

She lifted her head to meet his eyes. "In two years?" she asked. "I thought the Long Winter was three years away."

"It's going to take about a year to get everyone settled, so we plan to start early."

"Oh," she replied, laying her head back down on the pillow. She felt as if time was being stolen from her. They were already on a ticking clock where every second mattered, and this wasn't something she had planned for.

Sensing her despair, Vytas added, "We still have three years before we go in. You and I are in the last group."

No other words were said. They laid there, awake, lost in thoughts better left unshared.

****

Alice was in her lab when it happened.

She was delightfully lost in thought. Simultaneously excited about her new project and excited about her and Kyle. Things had been going well since his mining expedition concluded. He had found enough rare metals to build the power cells for the cryo-chambers and for the Cradles. Alice didn't let it bother her that he needed the success to bring him happiness. She was just thankful for it.

She was also anxious. Her brother was in the lab this week, and she had scheduled time to pitch her new idea to him. She hadn't seen much of Vytas during the last seven years. They were both busy doing their parts to prepare for the Long Winter. She wanted to catch up with him, but today wouldn't be that day. He was here as her boss, not as her brother.

No one else was in the clean room with Alice. It was blissfully silent except for her pounding heart. She was fully suited in the virtual reality gloves, manipulating her hands around something that wasn't visible unless you were wearing VR goggles. The strap of the goggles was squeezing her head, causing the "whoosh-whoosh-whoosh" sound in her ears.

She bit into her bottom lip, carefully moving invisible molecules, protons, neutrons. She was genetically modifying seeds to speed up their growth rate. This would enable them to plant crops after the Long Winter and quickly yield fruits and vegetables to replenish their food supply. If she could make this work for seeds, she hoped the process could be replicated in the animal embryos.

Without warning, the alarm began blaring rhythmically, and the blue strobe light on the ceiling began twirling. The obnoxiously loud mechanical horn caused Alice to wince and rip the VR goggles off her head, pulling strands of hair with it.

She squinted for a moment, as her eyes adjusted to the lighting in the real world. She watched as several people rushed by the glass separating the clean room from the rest of the lab. This wasn't the fire alarm; something else had happened.

Alice tossed the goggles onto the tabletop and then hurried toward the door, removing the gloves from her trembling hands. She reached into her pocket for her badge so she could release the door lock. *Where is it?* She checked her other pockets then glanced back to the workstation.

That's when she caught a glimpse. A familiar face was standing on the other side of the glass, peering in at her. It was Milo, her long-time assistant and friend.

Alice froze as their eyes met. In an instant, she knew everything was about to change.

She reached for her badge as Milo opened the door. "Alice," he said somberly. "You have to come with me."

She slipped her badge into her pocket and ran through the doorway.

****

"What happened?" Alice demanded as they hurried down hallway, toward the research and development lab.

"I don't know," Milo confessed. "There was an accident; that's all I know." He had been working with Alice for many years. He had also become a trusted friend, so it made sense the he would be the one to tell her the news.

"Is he —"

"He was alive when they sent me to find you."

"What was he doing?" she asked.

A crowd had formed outside of the research and development lab. Alice and Milo pushed their way through to the front. There was broken glass and blood on the tile floor. Alice lifted her hand to her mouth, holding in the scream that desperately wanted to come out.

"He shouldn't have been in here," Alice cried. "Not alone. He shouldn't have been in here alone."

"He wasn't alone," Milo said, as he waved at one of the security officers to come over. "This is Alice," he said.

"Who was with him?" she asked.

"Alice," the security officer said, placing his hand on her shoulder.

She couldn't breathe. She forced her eyes away from the bloody pool in front of her and met the kind eyes of the security officer for a split-second. Then she returned her attention to Milo.

"Milo, who was with him?" Alice demanded.

"Hanita was with him," he answered. "She went with him to the hospital."

She felt sick to her stomach. She couldn't feel her legs, but she was still standing between Milo and the security guard. She looked at the blood pool on the floor again. It was surrounded by a bright light that grew bigger and bigger, until all she could see was the blood.

"Come with me," the security officer said. "I'm going to take to you to him."

His voice was far away, muffled. She could barely hear him over the high-pitched whine in her ears. She tried to turn her head to look into his eyes, but it felt like she was weighed down.

"Alice. Alice, are you okay?"

She could hear Milo's voice, like he was on the other side of a wall. She started to turn her head toward his voice, and then everything went black.

Chapter 8

It had been nine years since the special summit and the announcement of the Long Winter.

The added crisp in the air was hardly noticeable at first. It began as a whisper, wet and raspy. A secret spreading like cheap gossip crept into the West, with all the stealth and purpose of an experienced hunter stalking its prey.

The air smelled of snow even before the first flakes fell from the sky. Winter was hiding in every shadow, lurking around every corner, just out of sight. It moved in softly, gently at first, not wanting to cause a disturbance. The gradual changes teasing the Westerners with still blooming flowers, green grass, and sunshine while reeking of despair.

Until finally, winter peeled back the veil of secrecy and revealed its true self. A chill that penetrated the skin, boring deep into the bones, came out of the shadows. The sun cowered in its presence and retreated behind a canopy of thick, gray clouds. Every breath inhaled pierced the lungs like ice-cold daggers.

The wind howled, spreading the news of the Long Winter. It whistled through gaps and shrieked along empty streets, tossing abandoned objects along with it. The ground hardened beneath the feet like cured concrete. And in its wake, a temperature drop that was so fast, the grass remained green under a thin sheen of ice.

Without warning, the drastic and sudden thrust into winter left trees still full of ice-covered leaves and flowers frozen in bloom.

And as the first flakes dropped from the sky, the Cradles were ready.

****

Alice was lying on her side, staring at the clock on the bedside table. She was willing the numbers to change so she could get out of bed and get her day started. She hadn't slept at all; too excited. Or was it nervous? Today was an important day, and she would be front and center.

Most people simply would have given up on sleep hours ago and just gotten out of bed, but Alice was a creature of habit. Schedules meant everything to her. Even if her body was unwilling, she was determined to stick to the schedule. A day without schedules was chaos.

Suddenly, the alarm came to life, disrupting the silence with annoying precision. 5:30 a.m. Finally.

Alice flung the sheet off her body and sat up on the edge of her bed. She dipped her toes into the shag carpet beneath her, sinking into the soft fibers. Then she switched off the alarm and put on her glasses. Smiling, she glided from the bed and made her way to the bathroom.

Her fingers brushed over the crisp, white lab coat hanging on the back of the bedroom door. She paused, drowning in thoughts of the year to come. Today, she would nestle the first survivors into their chambers to begin the Long Sleep.

The color drained from her face, and her smile faded as she continued into the bathroom and closed the door.

****

Alice was, by all accounts, a morning person, relishing all the details of a new day. She usually hummed while brushing her teeth; sang while showering; swayed while she hung her damp bath towel. Each new day brought excitement and unknown discoveries. But today, she only felt uncertainty.

She had immersed herself in work since the accident, trying hard to forget that dreadful day. It had put a strain on her friendship with Hanita. Alice had abandoned their regular lunch dates, as it was too painful. The accident should have brought them closer, but Hanita only reminded Alice of that day, and she didn't need a reminder.

Alice scowled while hanging her bath towel and wondered if she had made a mistake by volunteering to keep watch in Cradle Twelve. Would she go mad? As she straightened out the wrinkles, she managed a smile and thought, *That's better.* All of these things were part of the necessary order.

And even when she doubted herself or felt afraid, it was still important to stick to the routine. That's what she told herself.

She piled her wet hair on top of her head and slipped into her cotton bathrobe. She used the hand towel to wipe away the film from the fog-covered mirror. She leaned in close to the glass and examined her porcelain skin. It was dotted with tiny freckles high on her cheekbones and over the bridge of her nose. She looked at one in particular and wondered if it was new.

She leaned back from the mirror and turned on the water, adjusting the temperature to lukewarm. She washed her face and then applied a thin layer of moisturizer before putting her glasses back on.

****

Alice had taken the lead in drafting the Long Sleep protocols. It took time to put a human into stasis, so they decided to begin with nonessential persons first: the elderly and the children. Everyone else continued working on the construction of the remaining pods and bio-suits.

Some people who were sick had opted against the Long Sleep, as expected, and instead would help as long as they could and would not be moved into one of the Cradles. There would be no one to care for them medically, or in death.

Over the next year, the essential persons would be placed into stasis a little at a time, until only a few remained in each site to watch over them. These people were known as the guardians.

Choosing to be a guardian over the Long Sleep was a sacrifice some made willingly in order to keep everyone safe. Alice formed teams from this group and provided them with the necessary training so that each Cradle would be in good hands.

She entered the lab where the team leaders had already assembled, busily going through all of the system checks. She paused in the threshold, observing the activity before continuing to her desk.

She placed her clipboard on the table and then turned to address the room. "All right, everyone," she announced. "Can I have your attention?"

All the technicians in white coats stopped what they were doing, turning their focus to Alice. Some were seated, so they spun their chairs around to face her. Those who had been standing in front of other desks leaned against the tables and waited for her to speak.

"I'm assuming you've all met with your teams," she confirmed.

The room responded with nods and muffled "Yeses."

"Good," Alice approved. "I want to do a quick run-through one last time."

There were groans, and heads dropped.

"I know, I know," she said, pleading with them to settle down. "We've already done this so many times, but we only have one shot to get this right." She emphasized her point with her right index finger raised. She was a perfectionist, and they respected her for that. She leaned back against the table and motioned for Milo to take over.

With his tablet in hand, Milo moved to the center of the room and said, "Let's begin." He recited the sequence perfectly, not missing a single detail. Alice had been grooming him to lead a team, as he had also opted to be a guardian during the Long Sleep.

Since the accident, Milo had become more than Alice's assistant. He assumed more responsibility as she struggled to cope with her loss. He stepped up and took charge when she was unable to. He had become her best friend.

But if Alice learned one thing from the accident, it was that people have secrets. She kept Milo at a distance in order to protect herself. And she made sure they were not assigned to the same Cradle as guardians; she suspected that was what he wanted.

She was almost looking forward to the Long Sleep. She relished the thought of the solitude while watching over the survivors. And she hoped she would finally feel at peace.

Chapter 9

Hanita's eyes fluttered open. The room was pitch-dark, but her aching bladder was telling her it was time to get up. The windows in the apartment were boarded up now in preparation for the Long Winter. It was meant as protection in case of the glass breaking under pressure from extreme cold. This also meant that no natural light would creep in, which didn't matter anymore, since the sun had failed to make an entrance in about a year.

She lifted her head from the soft pillow and read the glowing numbers on the bedside clock. She was wrapped tightly in warm blankets, but it was 0625; time to get up. She reluctantly pushed the heavy covers aside and gracefully swung her bare legs over the edge of the bed.

She wrapped her arms around her body, trying to soothe the gooseflesh on her skin caused by sudden exposure to the cold air in the bedroom. Then she slid her feet around on the floor, searching for the slippers she had placed there the night before. Once her feet were snuggled safely in their warm sheaths, she paused on the side of the bed, gripping the edge of the mattress. She was holding herself up as she stared into the darkness, trying to wake up.

She finally stood up and rubbed her arms for warmth as she scooted around the bed and toward the bedroom door. She didn't need any light to find her way, so she hadn't clicked on the bedside lamp. One strap of her thin nightgown dropped off her shoulder as she felt for the robe hanging on the back of the bedroom door. As she lifted it off the hook, her hand brushed against the bio-suit hanging under it. She had almost forgotten.

She gripped the robe in her fist and pulled it to her chest. Standing there in the darkness, she lifted her other hand and rubbed the cold fabric of the bio-suit between her first two fingers and thumb. It felt like death.

She slipped her arms inside the plush robe before turning the doorknob. She walked into the hallway, gently pulled the bedroom door closed behind her, and finished tying the sash around her waist. As she made her way down the hallway, she glanced to her left into the second bedroom of the apartment, the office.

The door had managed to creep open again. A thin slice of overcast light was peeking through the boards nailed to the office window, just enough to show the way.

She tried not to look inside but couldn't stop herself. The second bedroom was painted a pale shade of gray, but in the right light, it resembled the most pastel shade of violet. This color was in beautiful contrast to the dark wood flooring.

There was a small desk in front of the window; an ergonomic chair was tucked neatly underneath. Sheer drapes framing the window had a leaf pattern in shades of gray that matched perfectly to the wall color. Artwork was placed neatly on shelves next to books. Photos and paintings were hung expertly on the walls.

Every detail of this room was perfect, and yet the beautiful, peaceful room filled her with an ache for something she never had.

She quickly looked away, picturing the cedar chest in the left corner of the room, just inside the doorway. In her mind's eye, the lid of the chest opened just enough to glimpse the contents: tiny clothes and blankets, handed down from her mother and hers before: A promise of a life that never came. She brushed away a single tear as she gripped the door handle and pulled the office door closed.

She slowly backed away and then continued to the right, into the bathroom.

****

Hanita flicked on the kitchen light and instinctively began making a cup of tea. She added water to the teakettle, placed it on the stove top, and clicked on the burner. Then she plucked a chamomile tea bag from the canister on the counter and fetched her favorite mug from the cupboard.

She knew she wasn't going to drink the tea; not today. She began her fast yesterday and had to remain on an empty stomach for her appointment later. But she was operating on autopilot.

While she waited for the water to boil, she looked into the living room. The heavy drapes were drawn closed, concealing the glass doors that led onto the quaint balcony overlooking the city. She hadn't been on that balcony since the snow began to fall.

The teakettle let out a soft whistle as the water reached a boil. She removed the steaming kettle from the burner and turned off the stove. Then she poured the hot water into the mug. The water began to turn amber in color as it swallowed the tea bag. She sat the kettle down and then lifted the string attached to the bag and proceeded to dip it in and out of the water.

The mug was warm in her hands, and the steam from the tea enveloped her face as she inhaled the sweet aroma. She shuffled farther into the living room, toward the glass doors hiding behind the layers of cloth and wood. She pushed the drapes aside and felt a rush of cold air sneak through.

Then she peered through an opening between the boards nailed to the door frame. She no longer recognized the ghost town below; it was once an exciting, bustling city. The sky was gray and cold now as they began the Long Winter. In five years, would she even recognize her home?

She remembered standing here with Vytas for the first time. She closed her eyes and imagined his arms around her. She could feel the warmth that surrounded their bodies as they stood there and admired the beautiful sunrise. The memory was so vivid; she believed she could smell him all around her, as if he was standing with her right now.

As she opened her eyes and looked through the small gap between the boards, she felt the memory slip away. Soon the West would be cloaked in darkness and blanketed under a thick layer of ice and snow. But she would never see it.

She closed the heavy drapes, walked into the kitchen, and poured the tea down the drain.

****

The technicians had finished their exam, and Hanita was left alone on the exam table behind the curtain. They had drawn her blood, taken her blood pressure, and recorded her temperature; all her vital signs had been checked and compared to what they had been six months ago.

She scooted off the table and began to slip out of the sterile gown, revealing her naked body. She tossed the gown onto the table and then reached for the black bio suit.

It was one solid garment; a full bodysuit meant to fit like a second skin. As she bent over, holding the bio suit in her hands, she pushed her long brunette hair out of the way over one shoulder. Then she stepped into the legs of the suit, one foot at a time, and began working the fabric up her calves, over her knees, and up her thighs. It seemed to move on its own as it stretched and hugged her curves. She continued wriggling into the suit, pulling it around her hips and up to her waist.

Then she slipped her arms into the sleeves, first her right arm and then her left. She tugged at the sleeves and then began moving the fabric farther up her torso. Lastly, she tossed her head back and pulled the suit onto her shoulders until, finally, she was all the way in.

She crossed her arms in front of her body and squatted a few times to comfortably adjust the suit. When she was finished, she stepped toward the privacy curtain and pulled it aside.

As she walked through the opening, she could feel the nanites crawling under her skin. Her body shivered and her spine tingled as the nanites pulled the zipper up her back to the nape of her neck.

****

The presence of the others in the brightly lit prep room had been indistinguishable from the furniture. But now, Hanita could feel them looming in every corner, whispering. This was the day she had been dreading. She wanted to disappear back behind the privacy curtain.

Alice was standing across the room by the plate glass window, her bright emerald eyes shining from behind wire-rim glasses. Her fiery amber locks surrounded her face like a halo, glowing off of her porcelain skin. She was squeezing a tablet close to her body, pressing it against her white coat, as she stood next to the door leading into the procedure room.

She smiled as Hanita walked toward her, but it was obviously forced. Hanita returned the gesture. It was an uncomfortable exchange for both of them. No words were said between them; they had already said everything they needed to.

Alice tapped on the screen of her tablet as the technicians attached wires to the built-in leads of the bio suit. Hanita stood still while they worked, silently watching them, with her arms lifted slightly at her sides. They were calling out words as they made the connections, and Alice would respond back each time with one word: "Go."

They moved quickly, without rushing. They must have done this a thousand times already, so it was more like they were moving efficiently than anything else.

One of the technicians said, "She's all set," after making the last connection, and then they both stepped aside.

Alice finished typing on her tablet and then looked up at Hanita. "It's time," she said, pushing her glasses farther up the bridge of her nose.

Mustering up the last bit of her courage, Hanita allowed her body to drift toward the door leading into the procedure room. She could see the silver tube waiting behind the plate glass window. Its door was open, inviting her in.

Alice stepped quickly in front of her and grabbed the door handle. She pulled the door open and stepped to the side, holding the door so Hanita and the others could walk through.

Hanita could feel the chilled air bite at her hands and her face as she left the prep room and entered the procedure room. Her tight-fitting iridescent black suit quickly adjusted to the change in temperature to keep her body warm. Remembering the matching gloves, she hurriedly unfastened them from her wrists and slipped her fingers inside. The gloves immediately began to regulate the temperature in her hands to the perfect 98.6 degrees.

As Alice closed the door and followed behind them, the two men in white lab coats led Hanita to the open chamber and motioned for her to step inside. When she pressed her back against the cushioned bedding, she noticed the chamber was actually reclined, maybe about 5 degrees. Not enough to notice while looking at it, but she could feel it as she lay her head back.

The men in lab coats slowly moved around her, blocking her view of the plate glass window. They began completing connections from the chamber to the wires attached to the suit she was wearing and making adjustments, all the while murmuring to each other. Their voices seemed so far away. Her chocolate eyes darted from one to the other, grasping at their words, but she couldn't focus. She couldn't catch what they were saying. It wasn't important.

Then she noticed the familiar blaze appear on her right side. Alice placed her warm hand on Hanita's cheek. "We're almost ready," she soothed.

Hanita nodded and asked, "Will I dream?"

"Close your eyes, and think about a time when you were the happiest." Alice's luminous skin seemed to warm the room by 10 degrees. "This is what you'll dream about," she promised, smiling kindly.

Hanita squeezed Alice's hand and breathed deep. "Alice —"

Alice gave her friend's shoulder a quick squeeze and then stepped away, out of sight, not allowing her to finish her sentence, not wanting to be reminded of the past.

For a moment, Hanita had forgotten about the two men in white coats. They had been there the whole time, hovering. Now, they quickly finished their work and left her alone in the chamber.

Hanita could feel her eyes becoming heavy, and her vision was starting to blur. *Not yet*, she thought to herself. She closed her eyes and saw Vytas. Images of him raced through her mind, his warm, caramel eyes and his strong whisker-speckled jaw.

She thought of their wedding day. He was wearing a dark suit and cobalt tie; the only time she ever saw him wear a tie, but she would never forget it. She remembered the bouquet of petite red roses he surprised her with that day. She thought of the day they met, the first day of the summit, ten years ago, when they first learned the Long Winter was coming.

"Why did you lie to her?" one of the men whispered to Alice as they stepped through the door and back into the prep room.

"We don't know for sure that she won't dream," Alice whispered back. "So I told her what she wanted to hear."

Hanita slowly opened her eyes one last time as she heard the door close. She was looking at the plate glass window separating the two rooms. She could see into the prep room, but the image was distorted. That's when she noticed that her eyes were wet.

A dark figure was moving toward her, closer and closer to the glass. She tried to lift her head for a better view, but it was so heavy. Was that Vytas looking back at her?

"Am I dreaming?" she wondered out loud.

The chamber whirred and hummed loudly as the door began to slowly roll up from its sheath until it met the other side. With a click and a hiss, the chamber was sealed. Hanita's eyes closed and did not open again.

****

Winter raged on, continuing its siege on the West as the Cradles filled up with hopeful survivors.

Wisps of white caught by the wind whirled through the air and settled into cracks, corners, and crevices, coating the ground with a thick layer of white powder.

Frost formed on surfaces, contagiously spreading its tentacles until everything was caught in its icy grasp. Sleet pelted the city, clacking against the windows. Ice cycles grew like roots from building overhangs, and tree limbs dropped like daggers to the ground below.

Bodies of water formed a fragile skin of ice that became stronger with each passing hour as the temperature continued to drop.

Wildlife and livestock had attempted to migrate out of harm's way, being pushed further west by the dropping temperatures. But vegetation was rapidly freezing over, and they were running out of food. It wouldn't be much longer before all life outside of the Cradles perished from starvation.

The power grid had failed in the East and in most of the North and South as well. Communications were completely cut off to these regions.

The longest day they had been dreading was here; they were firmly in the clutches of winter.

As the last survivors made their way into the Cradles, the West became buried in a thick blanket of snow. All that remained was a barren, crystalline wasteland, darkened by the imposing cloud bearing down on them.

The Long Sleep had begun.

All that was left to do was to wait.

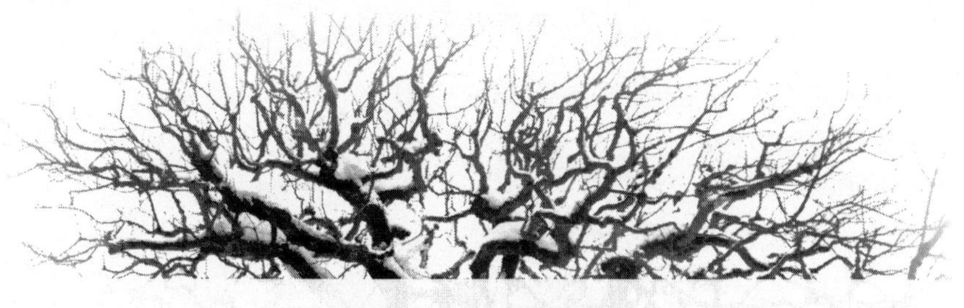

Chapter 10

The flashing red light was the only thing disrupting the darkness, illuminating a small corner of the lifeless machine. It blinked rhythmically, to an inaudible beat, until finally it stopped. Another light began to glow bright green, not blinking, though. Instead, this was a static light, indicating a full charge.

A black-gloved hand appeared from the darkness. One finger, illuminated by the soft light, extended from the hand and pressed the button next to the glowing green light.

The black-gloved hand brushed the coating of dust from the six-inch by twelve-inch screen on the machine. It blinked a couple of times as it came to life and made clicking and humming noises while the data began to load. When the boot-up routine was complete, the screen displayed six red buttons on a gray background.

The black-gloved finger moved across the buttons: [SETTINGS], [PROGRAM], [NAVIGATION], [MAPS], [PHONE], [VR REMOTE].

The finger stopped at the button that read [NAVIGATION]. The color of the button became a darker shade of red when pressed. A spinning blue circle appeared on the screen while the navigation page loaded, displaying more buttons: [PREVIOUS DESTINATIONS], [SEARCH], [ENTER DESTINATION], [LOCATE].

The finger pressed [LOCATE]. The spinning blue circle appeared again and then displayed three buttons on the screen: [VEHICLE], [PERSON], [DEVICE].

The finger selected [PERSON]. After the spinning blue circle disappeared, a keyboard was displayed on the lower portion of the touchscreen. On the top portion, there were two blank fields with labels beneath them: [Last Name], [First Name].

There was a blinking cursor in the [Last Name] field, indicating it was ready for input. The black-gloved finger extended to the keyboard buttons on the screen and one by one pressed the buttons: W-E-B-E-R

Then, the finger pressed the [TAB] key to move to the [First Name] field. One by one, the finger pressed the buttons: K-Y-L-E

The finger pressed [SEARCH], and the blue circle appeared on the screen, spinning for several seconds until it finally stopped and displayed a wide-view map. There were two locations pinned on the image.

On the far right, a blue push-pin labeled [YOU ARE HERE] was blinking. On the far left side of the screen, a red push-pin labeled [DR. KYLE WEBER] was blinking.

On the bottom of the screen, two buttons were displayed: [PLOT COURSE], [TRANSFER]

The black-gloved finger hovered over the first choice before eventually pressing [TRANSFER]. A command appeared on the screen that read [SELECT DEVICE], and two buttons were displayed: [REMOTE] and [OTHER]

The black-gloved hand reached down and picked up a black helmet from the dirt floor. The glow from the machine's touch screen reflected onto the glossy helmet as the figure stood and brought the helmet around in front. The figure, dressed in a heavy cloak of animal pelts over dark clothing, held the helmet with both hands before sliding it on.

Then, the figure extended one finger toward the machine and pressed [REMOTE] on the touch screen. The black-gloved hand felt down the side of the machine until it found a protruding object. The figure wrapped its fingers around the small device before releasing it from its holster. The screen on the device was lit up with one button: [START].

Holding the device in the left hand, the figure leaned toward the machine, extended one finger, and pressed [OFF]. The touch screen went dark, and the machine was silent. The only light was the glow from the handheld remote, illuminating the top of the machine just enough to make out the words on the label: "PROPERTY OF DR. KYLE WEBER."

The figure walked past the lifeless machine and commanded, "*Sledi mi.*"

Seven other figures emerged from the shadows, dressed in similarly heavy outdoor clothing, and fell in line behind the first one. Together, they climbed out of the tunnel of dirt and rocks, leaving Dr. Kyle Weber's mining robot behind.

Chapter 11

The passing years had peeled away all the comforts of routines and schedules. Alice no longer slept much, so she had no need for an alarm clock. She no longer greeted each day with excitement and anticipation. Each morning brought the same loneliness, and with every evening came dread for the next day. There was no order; only chaos.

Desperate to pass the time, she often found herself wandering empty hallways at odd hours. She was barely eating. Her once striking red hair was now dull and streaked with gray. She was ready for all this to be over. "Soon," she repeated to herself like a mantra. But for now, she had to make it through tonight.

It was almost 9 p.m. and seemed like a good time to snoop around. She found herself in Kyle's office. It was like a time capsule: Perfectly preserved, covered in dust and webbing from some of the only creatures to survive the Long Winter. She paused for a moment, honoring the memory of her old friend before pushing through the threshold into the past.

Kyle had been an avid reader, so there were a lot of books on the shelves. Escaping into a fantasy world was easy for him; reality was the challenge. Alice pushed her glasses up higher on the bridge of her nose. With one pale, boney finger, she grazed the spines of the uniform row of books. She breathed in the bouquet of the classic titles. They all looked the same except for one.

It wasn't in formation, like the other books, but rather lying on top, out of place. She snatched it off the shelf and felt the beautiful pattern all along the border of the leather cover as well as on the back cover. Engraved in remarkable detail was the image of a camel. She could feel and see the camel's hair, the intricate detail of the saddle and headgear. All created by hand, no doubt.

The book had no title, no author, but somehow, it seemed special. She opened the cover and read the inscription:

> To Kyle —
>
> I found this book in your mother's things and I think she would have wanted you to have it. She brought it back from her trip back east. She told me she had come upon a vendor selling books of hand-made paper, bound in leather; it was nearly dark. After careful consideration, she decided upon a book with a camel on the cover. The camel symbolizes sustenance and tolerance. They triumph over the harshest conditions and embody the spirit of endurance. Just like you, my son. I hope this book brings you peace. Love always, your father.

Alice remembered that Kyle's mother died when he was very young. He hardly spoke of her; he didn't seem to remember much about her.

She flipped the pages with her thumb, creating a slight breeze that fanned her long bangs. There were hundreds of pages of handwritten entries. "Kyle's journal," she gasped. "I'm intrigued." She slapped the journal closed as she exited the office, back into the cold hallway, and started walking toward her own quarters.

This would be an interesting night, after all.

****

Once in her room, Alice poured a glass of wine. She carried it over to the comfy chair in the corner, placed the glass on the side table, and clicked on the reading lamp. She lifted the blanket that was lying in the seat and then flopped into the cushion. Then she tucked her legs underneath her in the chair and spread the blanket over her lap.

She took a sip of wine and then replaced the glass on the table and opened the journal. She flipped past the foreword to Kyle's first entry.

Father gave me this journal as a gift for my tenth birthday. He said I should write in it every day.

Right away, Alice noticed there was no date for the entry; no date on the foreword, either. She flipped the pages through her fingers and confirmed there were no dates for any of the entries. *How odd*, she thought. She should be able to deduce the year based on what Kyle had written about, though. Undaunted, she continued to read from the beginning.

His childlike notes were very strange. He obviously had no idea what he should write about, but Kyle being Kyle, he was determined to make daily entries, as instructed by his father. He made observations about the weather, his schoolmates from grammar school, and notes about things he wanted. He was young, but even then, he knew he wanted to be a scientist.

As Kyle grew older, his handwriting began to change, and his entries gained maturity.

I met Alice today.

Alice recalled the day she met Kyle. It was the first day of their freshman year in college. He didn't look old enough to be there, still a gawky teenager. He was too skinny for his five-foot, eleven-inch frame and couldn't grow enough facial hair to make it worthwhile to buy razors. She also remembered how much of a gentleman he was and that she liked him right away.

I had coffee with Alice today. I wish I had the courage to ask her on a real date. I wonder if she would say yes?

Alice had no idea that Kyle had a crush on her back then. She thought of him only as a close friend in college. It wasn't until long after graduation, during the summit and after, when they began working together, that she started having different feelings for him. Why hadn't he acted on his feelings back in college? Why hadn't *she* acted on her feelings when they first emerged? She pushed those thoughts out of her mind and continued reading.

Alice has a new boyfriend: Chuck.

Alice snorted, spraying a bit of wine from her mouth as her whole body jolted. She hadn't thought about Chuck in a long time. They had fun during senior year of college, but it wasn't serious.

Graduation day!

That was a special day. Vytas was there to watch as she walked across the stage and gave the valedictorian speech. He seemed so proud of her. She kept staring at the two words on the page until the words became blurred as her eyes filled up with tears. She hadn't thought of her brother in a while; she tried not to.

She wiped her eyes and shook away the memories filling her mind as she continued reading.

> *Today I told Father that I do not want to follow in his footsteps and become a teacher. I want to pursue my master's in engineering. He's not happy.*

That was the day Alice met Kyle's father for the first time. She remembered seeing how proud he was of his son and wished that her parents had been there to watch her graduate. She also remembered seeing Kyle's father later that evening at the banquet; he appeared to be different, angry. She had wondered why, and now she knew. It wasn't anger; it was disappointment.

Alice also went on to achieve an advanced degree, but they did not attend the same university. During this time, she and Kyle grew apart. This is a part of his life that she doesn't know about. She read on about people he met, his studies and research, his first job. He wrote with pride about his breakthrough in cryonics.

> *The summit kicked off today, and I saw Alice. She is just as beautiful as she was in college.*

Alice remembered how they embraced that day and how good he smelled. They hadn't seen each other in years. Kyle looked so different, like a man. That was the day she began to feel differently about him.

She wondered why, after all their years apart at different universities and running into each other again as adults, Kyle was still unable to ask her for a date.

> *I had dinner with Alice tonight, just work. We discussed modifying the cryo-chambers, and she showed me her bio-suit. It's amazing!*

That was when Alice thought that maybe she could have a romantic future with Kyle. They began to spend a lot of time together after that day, but still, it never led anywhere.

> *Vytas approved my proposal to mine for rare metals in the amber zone of the Eastern Hemisphere. So much has to be done to prepare!*

Alice recalled that Vytas had sought out her advice before approving Kyle's proposal. He was reluctant, but Alice had agreed with the plan. That was right after Vytas and Hanita married.

> *Tomorrow is the first day of the amber zone mining expedition. I don't think I'll be able to sleep tonight.*

Knowing how things turned out, Alice wondered now if she should have advised Vytas against approving Kyle's proposal. Or, at least, insisted that he work with a team. He never should have run the mission alone. She saw that now.

> *I didn't expect success right out of the gate so I'm not discouraged. I will continue with my plan to check each pre-mapped quadrant. I know I'll find it out here. I have to.*

Kyle didn't do well with failure. He may have written that he didn't expect success right out of the gate, but really, that's what he needed. Coming up empty on day one sowed the seeds for catastrophe.

She read page after page of Kyle reporting "no luck" on his mission. She thought back to that time and how he spiraled into depression as each day left him empty-handed. This was also the time that Alice came to feel grateful that she had not pursued a romantic relationship with Kyle. She learned just how unstable he really was.

He was always one setback away from a complete breakdown, and Alice did not have the strength to pick up the pieces for him. She had decided it was best for her to be his colleague and his friend, nothing more.

> *It's out here, I know it. But what if it's just outside the amber zone?*

"What's this?" Alice wondered, jerking back and scrunching her forehead.

> *No one ever checks up on me ... If I were to stray a few miles inside the red zone, what's the harm?*

"Ugh," Alice moaned out loud. "Surely he didn't," she reassured herself. Not even Kyle would be that hell bent on success, would he?

> *Exploring the red zone is terrifying and exciting at the same time. If I get caught, I don't know what will happen. These are desperate times, and they need me. Besides, if I find the rare metals, it will all be worth it.*

"Oh no," Alice whispered. "He did."

> *Eureka!*

She stared off in the distance, thinking about that day Kyle burst into her lab. He was overflowing with excitement. She had been so happy for him. But now, reading this, she felt betrayed. He had lied to her; he lied to everyone. He risked everything for his success.

Then, Alice recalled that day when she woke him at his desk, after the expedition concluded. He was rude to her and tried to pass it off as sleep deprivation. Now she knew he was ashamed.

Feeling frustrated, she continued reading Kyle's words about the unapproved mining operation and then flipped to the next page. Her brow furrowed. This page was completely blank except for four words:

What have I done?

The handwriting was different, scared. A chill spread over her entire body as she stared at the four words scrawled on the page. What did it mean?

She flipped the page forward and then back, yawning widely. Then defiantly, she flipped forward through several blank pages until finally, there was another entry:

I can't stop thinking about Dara.

"Who the hell is Dara?" she hissed, suddenly feeling jealous. Kyle had never mentioned her.

I don't want to feel anything anymore. After several shots of whiskey, I went numb.

"Kyle started drinking over a woman?" Alice wondered. How sad that there was someone this meaningful in his life, and she never knew.

I'm having trouble concentrating at work. My thoughts stray to Dara. I can't sleep. Images of Dara invade my dreams. I feel like I'm losing my mind!

There was page after page of Dara, Dara, Dara.

The one person I want to talk to about all of this is Alice. But I can't ever tell her. I can't bear the thought of losing Alice, and I know I would if she ever found out the truth. Dara will be my secret.

Alice rubbed her forehead as she read. It was painful to read about Kyle's suffering. She had learned about the drinking, but much later. She had no idea it had started this far back.

I wish I had never gone to the red zone!

Kyle was expressing guilt and remorse, but why? Was Dara a colleague who worked with him on the mining expedition? Had it been Dara's idea to break protocol and explore the red zone? As far as Alice knew, Kyle had worked completely alone.

I can no longer outrun the reality of what I have done. I'm having nightmares all the time, while I'm asleep, while I'm awake. Nightmares about Dara.

As Alice read on, she realized this entry was the day before the accident. Did the accident have something to do with Dara? Alice touched her fingers to her lips and closed her eyes as she recalled that dreadful day. How the alarm sounded, Milo's expression on the other side of the glass, and the blood, so much blood that she fainted.

****

After Alice regained consciousness, the kind security officer escorted her to the hospital. She was outside of her body, watching herself walk through the automatic doors and wait by the reception desk while the officer spoke to the intake nurse. She could hear their muffled voices as the nurse tapped on her keyboard and read the information on the screen.

"He's in surgery now," the nurse said. "I can take her to the waiting room."

The security officer told Alice to go with the nurse. She would take her to wait with Hanita.

Alice watched herself walk away from the security officer with the nurse, through the security doors, down a brightly lit hallway. People dressed in hospital scrubs rushed by them. There were machines beeping and voices from behind curtains as they continued walking. The nurse opened a door on the left and led Alice inside.

Hanita was sitting in one of the chairs; she appeared to be unraveled. Some of her hair had become unpinned from atop her head. She wasn't wearing her uniform jacket, and it wasn't on the chair beside her. The sleeves of her white shirt were rolled up to the elbows and stained with crimson spots. She lifted her head, and her eyes met Alice's.

"I was there, Alice," she whispered. Her eyes were overflowing. "I saw it happen."

The words landed hard, and Alice suddenly felt numb again. She was no longer floating outside of her body. She had regained control of her legs and was telling them to move over to where Hanita was seated. She sat down and wrapped her left arm around Hanita's shoulder while her right hand squeezed her hand.

"It will be all right," she promised.

Hanita put her left hand on top of Alice's. "I'm so sorry, Alice," she said, sobbing. "There was nothing I could do."

They sat in silence for a moment, comforting each other. Alice felt like she had to hold it together for both of them. She always had to be the strong one. When her mother died, she had to pick up the pieces and take care of her father and baby brother. When her father died, she had to break the news to Vytas and take care of all of the arrangements. And now —

The door to the waiting room opened, and a nurse dressed in blue scrubs walked in. She removed a blue cap from atop her head. Her blonde hair was pinned up tightly, not a hair out of place.

"Are you the family?" she asked.

"Yes," Alice answered, sniffling as she braced herself for another devastating blow. "How is he?"

"He's out of surgery." The nurse walked over and sat in one of the chairs across from them. "He will survive his injuries."

Alice and Hanita both exhaled and squeezed each other's hands tightly.

"But I want to prepare you," the nurse continued. "There will be paralysis."

****

Alice shuddered in her comfy chair under the warm blanket as she remembered the nurse's voice saying the word "paralysis."

She folded the journal closed, saving the page with her bony finger, as she reached for her wine glass. She took a sip, letting the taste linger in her mouth before replacing the glass on the side table. She returned to the journal in her lap, opening it to the saved page.

She tried to continue reading, but it was no use. The memory of that day was stuck in her mind, and she kept replaying the same thing, over and over again. She removed her glasses and rubbed her eyes, recalling what happened next.

****

"Paralysis?" Hanita asked.

"Unfortunately, the injuries to the spine were severe," the nurse explained. "He will lose the use of his legs."

"He will never walk again," Alice confirmed.

"No, I'm afraid not," the nurse said softly. Her eyes were sympathetic. She managed a comforting smile as she placed her hand atop theirs. She seemed to be experienced at delivering this kind of news. "Are there any questions I can answer for you?"

"When can we see him?" Alice asked.

"He's in post-op right now, and they will be moving him up to the ICU," the nurse answered. "Once he's settled into his room, you will be able to visit him."

"Okay."

"I can take you up to the ICU waiting room now," the nurse added, standing in front of her chair.

Hanita and Alice slowly stood up together, not quite able to completely straighten their bodies. They were still holding hands; Alice still had her arm around her friend's shoulder. They followed behind the nurse to the door, leaning on each other for support.

The nurse opened the door so they could walk through and then quickly moved in front of them to lead them to the elevator. Alice floated outside of her body again and watched as the nurse pushed the up arrow. When the doors slid open, they followed the nurse inside, and she watched as she pushed the number eight.

The doors glided shut, and the elevator began to move. Alice watched the display above the doors as the floor numbers ticked by: two … three … four …

The elevator stopped, and the doors slid open to let two more people onboard. The doors closed, and the elevator began moving again: five … six … seven … eight.

The elevator stopped, and the doors slid open again. The other two people stepped aside while the nurse exited the elevator, Hanita and Alice in tow. Alice watched from above as they walked down a dimly lit hallway until they were at an open waiting area on the left. The nurse escorted them over to a couple of chairs and motioned for them to take a seat.

"Someone will be out to get you once Kyle is ready for visitors," she said before turning and heading back to the elevator.

****

Alice was now able to let the memory of that day fade away as she turned her attention back to the journal in her lap. That day changed everything for her. She wanted to speak with Hanita about the accident and why she was there, but things happened so quickly afterward. Alice was constantly working and visiting Kyle in the hospital. Hanita kept trying to reach out to her, but the more she tried, the more Alice pushed her away.

She remembered now that Kyle had asked her to bring him some personal items from home. He was in the hospital for several months before moving to the rehab facility. It occurred to her now that one of the items she brought him was this journal. She hadn't recognized it until just now.

> Father came to see me today. It was the first time since the accident.

That day was awkward. Kyle's relationship with his father was never the same since he had decided not to be a teacher. His father had always wanted that for his son. Alice wondered if Kyle's choice had anything to do with his mother. Would he have made a different choice if she were still alive?

> *Alice came by today. She comes by every day. She has no idea how much it means to me and how much I need her strength right now.*

Alice remembered that Kyle had been more like himself while he was in rehab. It was easy to visit with him, and she enjoyed it. There had been so much strain in their relationship before the accident; reading Kyle's journal revealed the reasons behind that: booze and Dara.

> *Today Alice brought me my laptop so I could start easing back into work.*

Alice recalled spending many long nights in the rehab facility after that. Once Kyle had his laptop, there was no stopping him. He had a lot of work to do and a whole team back at the lab waiting eagerly for his instructions. But he also had a long recovery ahead of him, and needed to focus on it.

> *Rehab is an angry bitch!*

Alice laughed out loud as she read the entry. Kyle had a lot of choice words for his rehab team; this was mild compared to other things he said. There was one particular technician who could really get under his skin. "What was his name?" Alice asked as she reached for her glass of wine. Not being able to remember, she decided to continue reading; maybe Kyle mentioned him.

> *The doctors told me today that I would never walk again. So I asked a friend to sneak in a bottle of whiskey, and we drank it together.*

Alice knew Kyle had started drinking while he was in rehab; she had always thought this was when it first began, though. Considering what he was going through, it did seem like a damn good time to start drinking, so she never gave him a hard time about it.

Now all she could think about was, *I wonder who brought him the bottle?* Maybe if he hadn't started drinking again, he wouldn't have spiraled into the darkness.

> I thought about Dara today. It was the first time since the accident. I need a fresh bottle of whiskey.

"Well, I guess it wasn't Dara who brought him the whiskey," Alice answered her own question.

> They offered me a motorized wheelchair but I rejected it. I don't deserve it. I rolled out of the rehab facility in a manual wheelchair. All I can think about is Dara. This is my penance.

Alice shook her head as she read that, and the word "penance" echoed in her mind. She wondered why Kyle felt the need to punish himself. He had his flaws, yes, but she didn't believe he had it in him to intentionally harm someone. And professionally, he was thriving. It was like reading a mystery novel; Alice was hooked.

> Being back to work has been challenging. My team is being very supportive, but now and then, I feel their pity-filled glances and hear the whispers. I could use a drink.

Alice had hoped that once out of rehab and back to work, Kyle would be able to give up drinking. She quickly realized that wasn't happening, and perhaps she now knew why. She was unaware at the time that he had felt so insecure. There was so much to do. She had been too wrapped up in her own work to realize that Kyle was spiraling.

> Today is the beginning of the Long Sleep. I am staying awake with Alice but with nothing to keep me busy, all I will be

thinking of is Dara. I might go insane, if I survive.

It became clear to Alice that Kyle was in love with Dara. They had formed a strong emotional connection that he depended on. Without her to talk to, he had lost himself. Now she understood his sadness, the isolation, the drinking, and the anger.

Alice had been reading for hours, so captivated by Kyle's journal that she hadn't been aware of the time. She glanced up for a moment and realized it was seven-fifteen in the morning. A memory of her once structured, fulfilling mornings briefly danced through her mind. She quickly pushed these thoughts away and dropped her eyes back to the book resting on her bent knees.

It was cold, so she pulled the wool blanket tighter as she snuggled deeper into the plush leather of the high-backed chair.

Alice is disgusted by me. I have no idea when I last wrote in my journal: yesterday, last week, last year ... I don't even care to know what day it is or when it is.

She read page after page of Kyle's loathsome words. How he appeared to hate himself and how he believed that she hated him as well. This was all going on while they were trapped together in the cold tomb that was meant to be their life boat. Right under her nose, during the time she had once romanticized as the time they would have the whole world to themselves.

She felt the tears well in her eyes and wiped her cheeks as they became wet. How did she miss this? How did she not see that Kyle was in so much pain? Was it true? Was she so disgusted by him that she didn't pay attention and didn't care?

She swallowed hard as she read the last haunting words in Kyle's journal.

I must return to Dara!

Chapter 12

[Beep. Beep. Beep. Beep.]

"Nooo," Kyle groaned. His head was throbbing, most likely due to the heavy amount of alcohol he drank the night before.

[Beep. Beep. Beep. Beep.]

The odor of booze and sweat wafted from the bedsheets as he rolled over and squinted with one eye at the menacing alarm clock. His mouth was stale, dry, and hot. Peeling his dry lips apart, he tasted the foulness in his mouth.

[Beep. Beep. Beep. Beep.]

He swatted at the alarm until it finally stopped and then closed his still squinting eye. What if he just went back to sleep? After all this time, after what he had done, would it make a difference?

He reluctantly pushed himself upright and then flung his legs over the edge of the bed. He heard the bottoms of his feet smack onto the floor, but he felt nothing. He scratched at his beard, thick and black like the curly hair on his head. Bits of white had managed to work their way in here and there, the price of time.

He yawned loudly and then grabbed the wheelchair beside the bed and pulled it into position so he could get in. His biceps and pectoral muscles flexed under the gray t-shirt he has wearing as he pushed up off the bed and lifted his body into the waiting wheelchair.

He'd had years of practice by now and was able to move himself in and out of the wheelchair without difficulty, even while drunk or hungover. In the beginning, he didn't have the upper body strength to do it on his own. He often thought how ironic it was that he finally had the muscle definition he'd always wanted, but he had nowhere to go and nothing to do. He felt like a prisoner.

One at a time, he lifted his lifeless legs until his feet were in position on the footrests. His legs were bare except for the white, wrinkled boxer shorts he had slept in. He could feel the chill in the room on his arms, but his legs felt nothing.

He rolled himself past the lab coat hanging on the back of the bedroom door and went into the bathroom.

****

Alice was no longer aware of the mechanical sounds of the ventilation system, the ticking of the clock on the wall, the computer on the desk; all sounds were being drowned out by the screeching alarm in her ears, repeating the same thing over and over: "I must return to Dara!" She stared at the words on the page, not really knowing what to make of them.

When did he write this? What did he mean? They hadn't communicated in years, not really, not about anything personal, anyway. Alice had never met Dara; they never worked together. She had never even heard of her. It didn't make sense. And what was the meaning behind the words, "What have I done?" scratched into the journal before the Long Winter?

Was this all the rambling hallucination of a drunk or something else? The thought was terrifying. Alice decided to confront Kyle and demand an explanation.

Just then, the silence was shattered by the rhythmic, buzzing alarm coming from the tablet on her desk. She tossed the blanket on the floor and slipped her shoes on. Then she stood up, Kyle's journal still in her hand, and walked over to where the noise was coming from.

She read the message on the screen and then swiped right to make it stop. Her brow furrowed as she read the information on the next screen and then she slammed the journal onto the table. She lifted up the tablet and placed it on top of the journal before picking them both up and heading toward the door.

As she charged through the hallway toward Kyle's quarters, more questions swirled around in her brain, and she grew angrier. She thought about the accident and how she'd felt sorry for Kyle after it happened. She gripped the journal and the tablet tighter as she realized Kyle had never told her the truth: That he'd been drunk that day, too drunk to have been fooling around in the R&D lab.

That it was his fault.

She tried to be understanding, like any good friend would be. When he wanted to quit rehab, she went with him and encouraged him to push himself. When he couldn't drag himself out of bed in the mornings to go to work, she rearranged her schedule to motivate him. And when he no longer wanted to enter the R&D lab, she understood.

She reached the door to Kyle's apartment in about two minutes, though it felt like longer. She paused for a moment, wondering if he was awake yet, and then pounded on his door.

****

Kyle had wriggled into a pair of gray sweatpants left lying on the floor. After he was finished in the bathroom, he rolled out toward the kitchen. The smell of coffee brewing filled the hallway. Thankfully, he had remembered to program the coffee maker last night before drinking himself to sleep.

There were empty liquor bottles on the breakfast table. He wondered what his mother would say if she could see the way he was living. He shamefully collected the bottles and tossed them into the trash bin. What he had become?

He grabbed a coffee-stained mug from the filthy countertop and poured a cup. He held the mug with two shaky hands and took a sip, no longer desiring the sweetness of sugar or richness of cream. There wasn't any in the apartment, anyway, and hadn't been for some time. He needed to eat something, but there was no food. Black coffee would have to do for now.

[Thump, thump, thump.]

"Damn it!" Startled by the knocking at the door, he burnt his tongue on the hot coffee. He put the mug down hard on the table and began wheeling over to the door. He had barely gotten the door opened before Alice began her assault.

"What did you do?" she demanded.

Any hope of acquitting him for his past mistakes had been left behind in the plush leather chair, under the warm blanket. Now, she only felt contempt.

"Wha—"

"Do *not* act like you have no idea what I'm talking about," Alice growled. "I read your journal, the whole damn thing."

Before he could respond, he had to raise his arm to protect his face as Alice hurled the journal at him. As he lifted the journal from his lap, he noticed his pants were wet. He had not felt it when the hot coffee splattered on his legs. He snatched up the blanket lying over the back of the chair next to him and began dabbing at the wet spots.

He rolled backward in his wheelchair, giving Alice space so she could enter the room. His head was throbbing and slightly lowered, in shame.

"Well?" She threw her arms out to her sides, hovering over him.

"Just keep your voice down," he said, motioning with his hand and grimacing as the throbbing in his head grew more pronounced.

"What the hell, Kyle"? Her face was scrunched up and red.

The rhythmic buzzing started again, this time in stereo. It was coming from the tablet she was holding at her side as well as from the one in the pocket of Kyle's wheelchair.

He looked calmly up at Alice, trying to neutralize her rage, and then abruptly suggested, "Let's finish this conversation in the lab." He started rolling toward her in an effort to get her moving.

The electronic noise seemed to soothe Alice, a reminder of her old, normal life, and her breathing began to slow. She knew she had work to do, something that needed their urgent attention. Kyle's trial could wait.

He continued slowly turning the wheels toward her and motioned for her to turn around. "Come on," he persisted. "Let's go see what this damn alarm is."

She turned and stepped aside, allowing him to roll past her. But he paused and motioned for her to start walking first instead. For a moment, they were in a standoff, neither wanting to concede to the other, both afraid the other would claim victory. She glanced beyond him one last time, wondering, before she gave in to her obligation then started walking toward the door.

They both seemed exhausted as they moved through the hallways. Kyle's eyes shifted in all directions, looking for an escape, as he slowly rolled the large wheels of his chair.

"Kyle, please just tell me you didn't jeopardize the whole mission." Alice's arms were swinging wildly as she walked. She looked down at him, waiting for his response, but he remained silent.

She shook her head. "You son of a bitch."

They turned left into the alcove leading into the lab. She reached for the handle and swung the door open, slamming it against the wall. As it bounced back toward her, she caught with her hand and held it there while he rolled in past her.

She released the door, and it closed tightly behind them as she followed him farther inside. She folded her arms tightly across her chest and stopped in the middle of the room. He had rolled all the way across the lab to his station at the console.

With his back to Alice, Kyle began, "I'm so sorry, Alice."

Those words felt like a knife piercing her heart. This would be much worse than she feared.

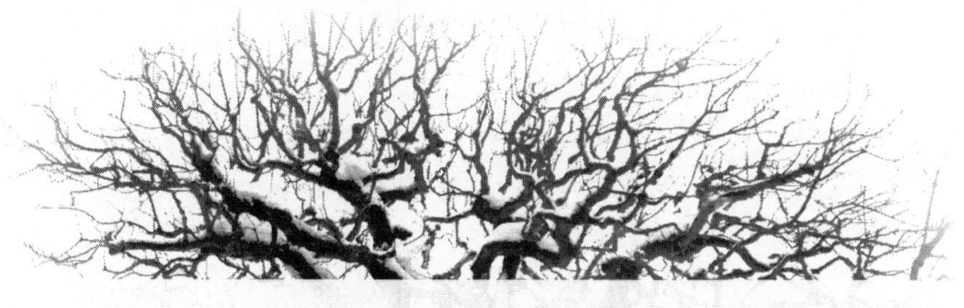

Chapter 13

"Will you shut it off?" Alice exclaimed. Usually just white noise fading into the background, the alarm was now more like a wailing infant, screaming for attention in the abyss created by Kyle's silence. She quickly turned to the left and examined the screens perched above the tables. Her eyes scanned up and down as she began turning to the right.

"There," Kyle said. He began pushing the big wheels, rolling toward the flashing red light. He lifted his hand and pushed the button, putting an end to the flashing light and beeping alarm. She walked up behind him and leaned on the table, over his left shoulder, as he typed on the keyboard.

They both looked at the monitor in front of them as lines of information appeared on the screen, scrolling up from the bottom.

"There seems to be a problem in one of the chambers." His words were slow as he read the details on the screen and punched more buttons on the keyboard.

"What is it?" she asked. For the moment, she had called a truce so they could do their jobs.

"Someone is ... dreaming," he responded, looking up at Alice in disbelief.

****

Vytas's eyes bounced back and forth behind his twitching eyelids, while images of a small boy drifted through his mind.

[*The boy was lying awake in his bed. Tiny hands emerge from under bed covers, and he rubs away the remnants of sleep from his eyes. It was early; he could tell by the way the light was cutting through the window covering.*]

["*Wake up.*"]

Vytas's eyes flickered open. He was lying on his back, in his own bed. He turned his head to find his wife, but her side of the bed was empty, covers pulled back. He turned his head back to the middle and closed his eyes as he inhaled the sweet perfume of pomegranates and cherries she left behind.

As he exhaled, the blurry blue image began pulling away. He tried to grab hold, but it unraveled, leaving him empty-handed once again. He was waking up.

He sat up and swung his long legs over the edge of the bed, wincing at the cold tile on his bare feet. He rested his forearms on his thighs and stared at the floor.

He looked sideways at the bio-suits hanging on the bedroom door, a glaring reminder that the Long Winter was upon them. So iridescent in certain light, the bio-suits shimmered with green and blue, but in reality, it was black and cold, like the bottom of the deepest cave.

He would eventually put the suit on, but not yet, not today. For now, he was wearing his gray boxer shorts and bright white t-shirt.

He lifted fluidly off of the bed and then made his way to the washroom. As he relieved himself in the toilet, he found it amusing to imagine what it would be like to piss inside the bio suit, or better yet, on it. How he would enjoy that. His breathy chuckle filled the small room.

After he finished, he pushed the button, and the liquid swirled out of the metal bowl. He examined his face in the mirror, wondering if he should shave. Hanita enjoyed the stubble, so he decided against it.

****

Alice pushed off of the table and stood upright, still staring at the screen. Then, looking down at Kyle, she responded, "That's not possible."

"See for yourself." He underlined the code on the screen with his finger so that Alice could confirm.

She leaned down again as she adjusted the glasses on her nose. She read the code and understood it to mean the same as what Kyle had deduced. Someone was, in fact, dreaming.

"It says here," she pointed at the screen, "the brain activity was detected in chamber number 19700702." She removed her finger from the screen and looked at Kyle. "Can you pull up the stats for that chamber?"

"Sure," he confirmed as he turned back to the monitor and typed on the keyboard. After a few taps, vital statistics for the person in chamber 19700702 appeared on the screen. "The brain activity is off the charts," he exclaimed, reviewing the data.

****

Vytas suddenly realized that he was washing his hands, though he was unaware of turning on the water. The voice from earlier still echoing in his head, he thought it was strangely familiar.

["*Wake up.*"]

He turned off the water and dried his hands. As he reached the doorway, he saw her. Hanita was across the room, standing with her back to him, flipping through a book on the dresser in front of her. The scent of chamomile wafted from the steam circling above the tea cup she held to her side. He paused there in the doorway to admire her. He folded his arms across his chest and leaned his solid shoulder against the door frame.

["*Wake up.*"]

The voice seemed closer now, like a whisper in his ear. His eyebrows contracted as he wondered, *Am I dreaming?*

[The boy peels the blanket away and scoots his legs off the side of the bed until his feet reached the floor. One leg of his blue pajama pants was curled up to his knee.]

"You're not fooling anyone," Hanita teased, singing.

This day was familiar, but it was different. The voice and the boy kept appearing in Vytas's mind, but who was he? He heard Hanita's voice and remembered responding back to her, "Am I that obvious?" but the words were not coming.

****

"Look at the heart rate," Alice said, pointing at the screen, drawing Kyle's attention to the data. "It's fluctuating between 140 and 180 beats per minute."

"This person is experiencing tachycardia," he confirmed.

"Is it a nightmare?" she asked.

He shrugged, looking helplessly at the monitor.

****

Vytas was confused. It was as if two memories were overlapping: One he could remember, but the other was unfamiliar. The boy …

["*Try harder*!"]

Vytas's head flung to the right, and then with a jolt, his head flung all the way to the left. Beads of sweat appeared on his crinkled forehead.

"Perhaps I'm just that good," Hanita said, giggling, playfully wiggling her hips.

[The boy sneaks clumsily across the bedroom and presses his ear against the back of the bedroom door. He brushes strands of light brown hair from his caramel eyes as he steps back from the door.]

Vytas struggled to remember what happened next. He asked Hanita what had her so captivated. That's right, and then she said —

["*Wake up*!"]

Louder now and more demanding, the voice stung at the back of Vytas's neck. He groaned as he struggled between sleep and awareness. He remembered saying, "Do you remember the day we met?"

[The boy grasped the shiny handle with both tiny hands and slowly, quietly, pried open the heavy door, using all of his strength. Then he slipped through the opening before the door closed behind him.

["*They're coming.*"]

The voice was very clear this time and frightened.

Vytas's eyelids sprang open; he was awake.

****

Alice turned around and bounded to the other side of the lab. She plopped down in a chair, rolled under the desk, and then slid the keyboard closer and started typing loudly. Information began to appear on the screen in front of her. "What was that chamber number?" she yelled back to Kyle.

"1-9-7-0-0-7-0-2," he answered.

Alice typed the numbers one by one as Kyle called them out, pressed enter, and waited a moment.

Suddenly, another alarm, different than the first one, screamed out in the lab. Alice turned around, back toward Kyle, to see a flashing red light on the console. Kyle pounced on the keyboard and quickly pressed some keys.

"No, no, no," he said, sounding worried "This isn't possible."

"What's happening?" she asked, pushing away from the desk and standing up from the chair. Waiting for him to answer, she noticed a faint beep from the monitor behind her. She turned back and leaned down to read the screen.

"This is Vytas," she gasped.

"Alice," Kyle said as he looked back, trying to get her attention. "The chamber is open."

Chapter 14

Vytas was upright in the chamber and remained still as he watched the chamber door roll open. He blinked his eyes several times, trying to clear the haze of the Long Sleep. *Was I dreaming?* he wondered to himself.

The last thing he remembered was Alice's sweet face before watching the chamber door close. He remembered the hissing sound it made as it sealed. He remembered his ears popped as the chamber pressurized. *How long ago was that?*

He searched the room with eyes. *Where is everyone?* He was confused and worried that something had gone wrong.

He lifted his right arm and felt his chest for the leads connected to the bio-suit. One by one, he disconnected them. Remembering the leads attached to his temples, he then reached up and peeled them from his skin.

Physically, he felt great: well rested, nourished, regenerated. He felt like he was waking up from a good night's sleep. He didn't expect to feel this way after waking from the Long Sleep, even though that is exactly what was promised. But he also didn't expect to wake up alone.

He pushed off the back of the chamber with both hands and stepped out with his right foot. He hesitated there for a moment, listening and looking, before pulling his left foot out. He turned his body left and right; there were rows and rows of silver chambers in both directions and in front of him. He stepped to the right, past the chamber he had been resting in, then turned to look at the back of the room. More rows of silver chambers. From this vantage point, he could see they were all still sealed.

He turned to face the front of the room and saw a blurry figure coming toward him. The room was dimly lit, so he took a few steps forward in an effort to see more clearly. As the figure moved closer, it became clear that it was not Alice, or Kyle, for that matter.

A child, he thought, as he doubted his own eyes. He lowered his head as the barefoot boy in blue pajamas stepped closer, until he finally stopped just a few feet in front of him. Was this the same boy? Was that a dream? *Am I still dreaming?* he wondered to himself.

He crouched down on one knee and looked deep into the boy's caramel eyes. He reached out with his right hand and stroked the boy's sandy blond hair in an attempt to confirm he was real.

"Hello," Vytas said softly.

The boy smiled back and replied, "Hello."

****

Alice hurried over to Kyle's station, their previous conversation now on pause. "Pull up the live feed in the chamber room," she ordered.

Kyle pushed buttons on the keyboard in front of him until the image on the screen changed. They could now see inside the chamber room and everything looked normal.

"Show me chamber 19700702," she said, tapping the monitor.

He pressed more buttons and used a lever to adjust the camera position and zoom in on the chamber where Vytas had been sleeping.

"There," she pointed and leaned in. "Zoom in closer."

The chamber door was open, and Vytas was awake and removing leads from his bio-suit. They watched as he cautiously stepped out of the chamber, obviously confused, turning his body right and then left. He stepped to the left of the frame and then just stood there.

Vytas turned to the front again, facing the camera, and appeared to be focused on something that was out of frame. His head was slowly lowering, as if something, or someone, was approaching.

"What's he looking at?" Kyle wondered out loud.

Alice was squinting at the screen and shook her head. She grasped the lever from Kyle and zoomed in closer, trying to get a better picture.

They watched as Vytas crouched down on one knee and reached out his right hand. Alice tried to adjust the camera angle to see what he was touching, but the camera wouldn't tilt any lower. She slammed her hand on the desk, frustrated. They watched as he stayed like that for a couple of minutes.

"Is he talking to someone?" Kyle asked.

****

"What's your name?" Vytas asked.

"Liam," the boy responded, flashing a big smile back at the older man, revealing a mouth full of teeth changing from baby to adult. "We have to go," Liam said. "They need your help."

That voice. Vytas's hair stood on end, and he raised his right eyebrow, studying Liam closely. So much information was coming at him all at once; too much. He lowered his head, feeling the air being pushed out of his lungs like a punch in the gut. He needed time to process what was happening: How long had he been asleep? Why was he the only one to wake? He lifted his head and looked into Liam's big eyes.

"Who needs my help?" Vytas asked.

Liam shrugged his tiny shoulders and answered, "They're coming."

Vytas could no longer hear the hum of the chambers around him, just a piercing tone in his ears, growing louder and louder. He clenched his jaw tight and slowly rose to his feet.

He reached out his left hand, and Liam took hold of his fingers. He folded his fist closed, swallowing up the boy's tiny hand, and they began walking to the front of the chamber room.

"Where are we going?" Vytas asked.

"To find Alice."

****

Alice and Kyle helplessly watched as Vytas lowered his head for a moment before standing again and walking out of frame.

"Where is he going?" Alice asked out loud.

Kyle began slowly rolling backward, away from the desk, as Alice took control of the keyboard. She was desperately trying to pull up a camera angle that would capture Vytas and whoever he was with. She leaned in closer, only able to catch passing glimpses of Vytas, but never able to see his companion.

Suddenly, Alice heard a noise behind her and turned to see Kyle positioned in front of the center station. His hand was on top of the large red button that controlled the lock on the lab door.

"No, wait!" she yelled.

"Whoever he's with is not coming in here," Kyle insisted as he slammed his palm down on the button.

****

Liam led Vytas between the rows of silver tubes to the double doors, where they exited the chamber room. They turned right into the darkness.

Motion sensors triggered the lights as they walked, illuminating the main hallway as they advanced deeper into the center of the Cradle. Vytas realized that Liam was taking him to the lab.

They stopped in front of the alcove leading into the lab, about five feet from the door. Vytas looked down at Liam, as if he was awaiting instructions.

"Alice is in there," Liam said, releasing the man's hand and pointing at the closed door. "They need your help."

****

Alice and Kyle were unable to track Vytas's movements once he left the chamber room. Since it was only the two of them in the Cradle, they had disabled the cameras in the main hallways years ago and could only turn them back on from main security.

They scanned through images captured by cameras in various alcoves but were unable to get a glimpse of him until he approached the lab. They weren't able to see him on the monitor, but the motion sensor was tripped, lighting up the alcove.

"He's right outside," Alice exclaimed, looking back over her shoulder. She quickly turned her attention back to the monitor and pushed buttons on the keyboard, trying to move the camera.

****

Vytas stepped toward the door to the lab and reached for the handle.

"The door is locked," Liam replied.

Vytas stopped and looked back at Liam, his right arm returned back to his side. *How did he know the door was locked?* he wondered.

"Kyle locked the door," the boy said.

"Is he in there?" Vytas asked, motioning toward the door.

Liam nodded his head up and down.

****

"Something's wrong, "Alice grumbled, jabbing her finger at the buttons on the keyboard and growing more and more frustrated. "The camera won't move."

"The motor went out on it a few weeks back, and I haven't fixed it yet," Kyle confessed. "We will have to wait until he comes closer to the door."

Suddenly, they saw Vytas step into the frame and reach for the door handle. The camera was positioned up high in the corner of the alcove and was aimed down at the intercom. They were only able to see directly in front of the door.

"There!" Alice pointed at the monitor to get Kyle's attention. He rolled back over to the desk and watched the monitor with Alice.

Vytas stopped and lowered his arm, looking back over his right shoulder.

"Why did he stop?" Kyle wondered, his hands outstretched.

They were able to see the top of Vytas's head and a sliver of his jawline, but not his face. From the camera angle, it was difficult to tell what was happening outside the door; there was no sound, but he appeared to be speaking and gesturing with his left hand.

"He's talking to someone," Alice realized. "Is someone else awake?"

****

Vytas again turned his attention to the door. There was no glass panel, so he was not able to see inside. To the left of the door was an intercom. He stepped sideways and pushed the button on the intercom so he could speak to them.

"Open the door, Kyle." Vytas's tone was calm but unconditional. He released the intercom button but his hand remained hovering over the box.

His chest was heaving and he was looking at the floor. He waited but the door did not open.

Vytas pushed the intercom button again. "Kyle." He leaned his head on his arm and repeated, "Open the door." He turned his head to the side, still resting on his arm. This was all so confusing. He was following the instructions of a child who may only exist in his mind. Or this could all be a dream.

His eyes became fixed on the camera in the north corner of ceiling. He knew Kyle was watching, so he looked directly into the lens and pushed the intercom button. "I will get the door open, Kyle." He released the button and turned to face the camera, adding, "Count on it."

He looked around for something he could use to open the door. There was a utility closet just across the hall. He looked down at Liam, still standing in the hallway in front of the alcove.

He placed his hand on the boy's shoulder. "I'm going right over there." He tilted his head to the right, toward the utility closet door. He gave Liam's shoulder a gentle squeeze and raised his eyebrows. "I want you to stay here, okay?"

Liam looked up with his big eyes and smiled back, nodding high and low just once.

Vytas moved quickly to the utility closet and opened the door. He felt around for the light switch while he held the door open. The light was bright and revealed mostly cleaning supplies: broom, bleach, towels. He reached inside and pushed items around on the shelves. Plastic bottles fell to the floor.

When he looked down to kick one of the bottles back inside the closet, he spotted the axe leaning in the corner. He reached down with his right hand and lifted the axe. Still holding the door with his other hand, he choked up on the handle to get a better grip. His muscles were contracting under the weight of the axe; the bio-suit had done what it was meant to do during the Long Sleep.

****

Alice watched on the monitor as Vytas turned from the camera, his back to the lab door, and looked left and right in the hallway.

Kyle rolled over behind her after locking the door. "He sounds a little pissed," he whined.

"I wonder why?" Alice replied sarcastically. She wanted to say, "Maybe it has something to do with suddenly waking up and being locked out of the lab where the only other two non-sleeping humans are." She thought it was better not to say anything, considering how mad she still was.

Without warning, Vytas looked down and reached out in front of him before he walked out of the frame.

"Damn it," Alice shouted. "Where is he going now?" She slammed the keys on the keyboard, but it was no use; the camera in the alcove would not move.

"What was that?" Kyle asked, pointing at the monitor.

"What was what?" Alice asked, squinting, trying desperately to see what she missed.

"There was a flash of light, over there," he explained, pointing to what was in the main hallway to the right of the alcove. They watched as shadows flickered on the monitor. After about a minute, they both saw the beam of light become slowly extinguished, leaving behind only the overhead glow of the hallway lights.

"Where is he?" Alice demanded.

They continued staring at the monitor, waiting for Vytas to reappear. Then, something flashed past the camera, swinging fast in a downward motion.

****

Vytas backed out of the utility closet and let the door close behind him. He looked toward the lab; Liam was obediently standing in the same spot, in front of the lab door. He walked over and knelt in front of the boy so he could look him in the eyes. He let the axe rest on the floor next to him.

"Will you do me a favor?" he asked, winking.

"Yes." Liam hopped slightly, eager to help.

"I want you to be safe," he said, touching his strong hand to Liam's tiny chest. "Will you stand around the corner while I get this door open?"

Liam nodded and said, "Okay."

"Good." Vytas grinned and nodded back. "Hurry."

He watched as Liam turned and ran to the hallway junction, about twenty feet away. The boy paused there, looking back.

"Go on," Vytas said, motioning with his hand for Liam to continue around the corner, and he watched until the boy was out of sight. Then he gripped the axe handle and rose to his feet, slowly turning his attention to the lab door.

He stepped closer, the axe hanging by his side. With his knees slightly bent, he swung the axe backward over his right shoulder. He gripped the handle with both hands as he brought the blade down fast and hard on the door handle, with a loud clank. The impact created sparks and caused the axe to recoil slightly.

The door handle was severely damaged, but the lock was still intact. Vytas let out an audible grunt with the next powerful swing. The door handle crashed onto the floor and slid down the hallway. He hurled his body at the door, propelling it open.

Still brandishing the axe, he wiped away the trace of sweat from his upper lip with the back of his hand as he sauntered into the room. There was a work table in the center of the lab, to the left. Alice was just ahead of him on the other side of the center table.

She was facing Vytas, braced up against the desk; he almost didn't recognize her. Dull, white streaks extinguished the fire in her once-flaming locks. Her radiant skin had been suffocated by time. She appeared unharmed but was frightened.

Kyle was seated in his wheelchair about ten feet away on Vytas's right, to the left of Alice. He was rolling backward and looking just past Vytas.

"Who is with you?" Kyle asked.

An image of the fair-haired boy with the big, caramel eyes flashed through Vytas's mind. "No one," he answered, shrugging. Liam would be his secret.

"How did you wake up?" Alice asked as she ran to Vytas. No longer able to control her relief, she wrapped her arms around her brother's neck. He hugged her tightly with his left arm, still holding the axe in his right hand. She felt different, thin and frail. How long had it been for her?

"I don't know," he lied.

"You're just in time, brother," she said, stepping back and wiping tears from her cheek. "Kyle was about to confess."

"Confess what?" Vytas asked, glaring at Kyle.

"Go on, Kyle," Alice prodded. "Tell him about the red zone and about Dara. Tell him the truth about why you had your accident.

"What's this about the red zone?" Vytas asked, watching as Kyle squirmed in his chair, searching for the words. "What the hell has been going on, Kyle?"

"Let me explain," he began.

As Kyle cleared his throat, Vytas's eyes shifted to the orange flashing box on the monitor nearest to Kyle. "What is that?" he demanded, pointing at the monitor.

Kyle glanced over his shoulder at the monitor on his right and then looked back at Vytas. "It's the exterior motion alarm," he replied, swallowing hard.

"That's impossible," Alice snapped, shoving Kyle aside to see for herself. Now in front of the monitor, she read the warning message flashing on the screen. She tapped a few keys on the keyboard and brought up an image on the screen from an external camera. The image changed as she continued to tap, revealing views from other cameras, until finally —

"Look here," she announced, pointing at the screen.

They all watched as several figures walked into frame, cresting over a nearby hill. They were dressed for the cold, wearing helmets that shielded their faces and heavy patchwork cloaks made of what appeared to be animal pelts. Dark clothing covered their bodies.

Vytas tapped the screen and switched the view to a camera just outside. They watched intently as the group walked closer, approaching the entrance to the Cradle.

Vytas remembered the words spoken to him in the dream. The boy wearing the blue pajamas relayed a warning. Perhaps it was a premonition? The image of the fair-haired boy with the sweet caramel eyes appeared in his mind, and he kept repeating the words over and over: *They're coming.*

He adjusted the image on the monitor and watched the tall, green grass as it whipped back and forth in the gusting wind.

Winter was over.

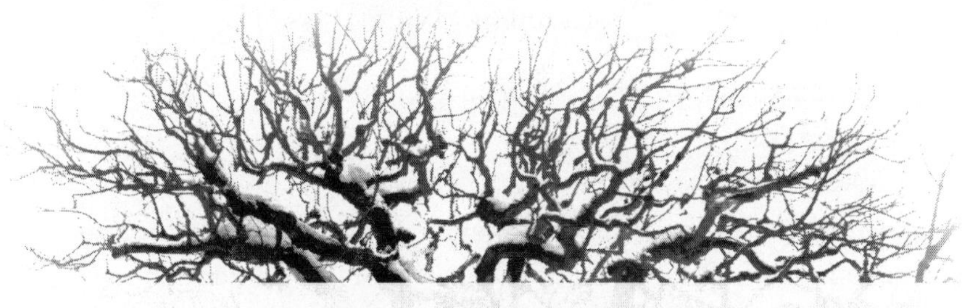

Chapter 15

"How soon can we wake everyone?" Vytas asked. He was leaning over the monitor mounted into the center table now, watching the figures walk closer.

Alice sighed, her mouth agape. "The protocol was designed to begin automatically, but only for members of our team." She looked to Kyle for assistance in providing a more complete answer.

"Correct, and not for another … " Kyle tapped on the keyboard and pulled up the schedule, answering, "Two weeks." He turned to face Vytas before adding, "We've been periodically adjusting the date as the Long Winter dragged on."

"Can you override the protocol?" Vytas interrupted. He touched his hands to his head and inhaled deeply as he turned to face Kyle and waited for the answer he knew he wouldn't like.

Kyle pursed his lips and tilted his head to one side. "Yes," he said after some hesitation, "but it will take both of us." He pointed at himself and Alice. "Once we have two team members awake, we can work a little faster, but still —"

"That's not fast enough," Vytas finished Kyle's sentence. His leaned his head back and began to pace in the lab, searching for a solution. He woke so easily from the Long Sleep, or at least it seemed that way. In reality, he had no idea how long the process had taken; hours, minutes?

Alice noticed movement on the panel in the center table. She stepped closer and enlarged the image.

"They're trying to open the door," she growled.

Vytas spun and hurried back to the table to see for himself. He turned his head to the left to face Kyle. "Do you know anything about this?" he snapped, remembering what Alice had said: that he was just in time for Kyle's confession.

"What? No," Kyle responded, confused.

Vytas's resolute gaze, bleeding with distrust, held Kyle's eyes. "You were about to tell me something earlier," he began. "Something about the red zone."

"I swear," Kyle cried. "I don't know."

Even as the words passed his lips, Kyle wondered if he was telling the truth. Did he know anything about the visitors? Had he done something that brought them to their threshold? Did it have anything to do with Dara? He couldn't let Vytas know that he doubted himself, so he said nothing more. He remained confident in his eye contact.

"Guys," Alice pleaded softly, pointing at the screen.

Vytas walked up behind her and leaned in while Kyle rolled toward the monitor. They both read the words on the screen.

"They're decoding the door lock," Vytas confirmed. His clenched eyebrows cut deep creases in his forehead as he realized the lab, with the broken door handle, was no longer safe. He slowly turned to face Alice. "I want you to find a safe place and stay there."

She defiantly shook her head and backed away from Vytas. "No way," she said. "You are not doing this alone. I just got you back."

Vytas dropped his head and tightly squeezed his eyes shut. He knew he needed help, but he had to protect his sister.

"You're right," he conceded, raising his head and looking softly into her dewy green eyes. "We will have to work together." He looked back down at the panel, watching as another number in the door lock was decoded.

"We don't have a lot of time," Vytas said. "You and Kyle hurry to main security and lock yourselves in."

"No," Alice said.

"Alice, please." He reached for her, but she refused his touch.

"I won't leave you." Her eyes began to swell with tears.

"You'll be with me," he said. "I need you to be my eyes, and main security will give you the best vantage point."

Alice thought this over while Vytas jogged to the other side of the room, by the lab door, and reached into a drawer. He pulled something out and then returned to Alice. He was holding a set of two-way communication earpieces. He handed one of them to Alice while he pressed the other into his right ear.

"There's only one way in," Vytas said. "I have no doubt that they have studied our facility; they didn't come all this way without being prepared." *Where did they come from?* he wondered.

Alice gave in and pushed the earpiece into her ear.

"They will enter from the north door," Vytas explained, "and continue down the main elevator. I need you both to be watching the monitor and tell me how many enter the elevator."

Alice and Kyle both nodded in agreement.

"Where will you be?" she asked.

"They will exit the elevator on this floor." Vytas looked firmly into Alice's eyes. "And I'll be waiting."

****

Alice and Kyle entered the main security room and secured the thick door behind them. The room was dark except for the glow of the monitors and colored buttons on the main console. She hurried to the desk and sat down while Kyle rolled up next to her.

She pressed the button on the earpiece so she could talk. "Vytas, can you hear me?"

After a short pause, he answered back, "Yes, I can hear you."

She slid a keyboard closer and started tapping on the keys. She watched the monitors come alive one by one as she switched on the hallway cameras they had previously disabled. She continued typing and watched the images change until finally, she was able to see the view from the north entrance on the surface.

"Are you in main security?" Vytas asked.

"Yes," she confirmed. "I've pulled up the image from the surface camera —"

Her words were interrupted by a wailing alarm, indicating the entrance to the Cradle had been breached.

"Kyle," Alice yelled, spinning around in her chair. "Turn it off."

"What is that?" Vytas asked.

Kyle tapped furiously on the keyboard until the screeching finally stopped. He turned to Alice and nodded.

"Alice," Vytas whispered.

"I'm here," she answered. "They're inside." She hesitated as she watched for movement on the monitors. "I don't see anything yet."

"Disable the motion lights in the hallways," he ordered.

"Okay," Alice agreed. "Kyle, he wants you to disable the motion lights."

Kyle had been simultaneously typing on the keyboard in front of him. "On it," he said.

"We're working on it," she repeated to Vytas.

She continued typing on the keyboard and pulled up the image of the foyer, just inside the north entrance. She was just in time to see the elevator doors close. She pointed to the monitor in front of her, showing Kyle the illuminated down arrow next to the closed elevator doors.

"Vytas," Alice hissed. "They're heading your way."

****

Vytas ran through the elevator foyer, past the six sets of silver doors and around the corner. The foyer was still brightly lit, but he could still clearly see the glow of the down arrow, indicating an elevator was on its way. He was guessing they would exit the elevator and turn left, either to the lab or the chamber room, so he positioned himself to the south, on the right of the elevator. The visitors would have to travel one hundred feet underground before reaching the chamber floor.

He leaned his right shoulder against the wall in the hallway, tightly gripping the axe handle with his right hand, and watched the center elevator doors across from him. Before leaving the lab, he snagged the sash from one of the lab coats and wrapped it around his left hand. Weapons were in the armory on another floor, so he had to make do with what he could find.

"Got the lights," Alice announced in his ear, just as the hallway and elevator foyer went dark.

Vytas, still cloaked in the black bio-suit, blended into the shadows now. His heart thumped in his chest as he waited for the elevator to land.

"Vytas, I have the image up in the elevator foyer," Alice said. "We've adjusted the camera lens for night vision."

"Count them as they exit the elevator," he said.

"All right," she replied.

"I will move in once they are all out. I need you to follow them on the monitors, Alice. You have to be my eyes."

"I will." She nodded her head as she agreed.

Alice turned her head to the right to face Kyle and muted the earpiece microphone.

"Can we control the doors from here?" she asked.

"Yeah," he said, tapping on the keyboard and pulling up a diagram of the floor that showed all the doors. "What do you have in mind?"

"I've set up the hallway cameras for night vision, so we can easily follow them." She looked at Kyle's monitor as she spoke. "Keep that up on your screen and be ready."

[*Ding.*]

She whipped her head to the left as a bell rang from the monitor in front of her. The elevator had arrived.

"Vytas," she whispered.

****

[*Ding.*]

The obvious indication that the elevator had landed pierced the elevator foyer. Vytas stepped slightly backward, hugging the wall, until he was swallowed completely by the black hallway.

"I know," he responded. "They're here."

His eyes had adjusted to the darkness. Vytas watched as the elevator doors slid open, illuminating the foyer. A figure emerged from the elevator. It looked to be male, but it was impossible to tell through the thick layer of animal pelts. His face was obscured by the helmet with the black tinted shield.

The figure took another step out and then turned to his right, toward Vytas, and paused. He appeared to be carrying a weapon of some kind. Vytas could make out a cross-body strap attached to the weapon but the guard was holding it across his chest as he scanned the elevator foyer, looking for signs of life.

Vytas pressed his back against the wall, staying out of sight, and waited for Alice's voice.

****

"That's one," she whispered. She was perched in front of the monitor showing the elevator foyer, watching the cloaked figure. His head turned slowly to the left, scanning the foyer. After a few seconds, he motioned to the group in the elevator.

"Two, three … " she counted softly as they stepped out, one by one, without speaking a word and turned to their left, just as Vytas expected. Each figure was dressed in similar heavy garments and helmets, just like the first one. They each turned quickly as they exited the elevator, making it difficult to determine their gender. It became clear that only the one standing guard, the first one, was holding a weapon.

"… four, five," Alice continued counting as they walked past the first figure. He was still standing watch, his head on a swivel, scanning the elevator foyer.

"… six, seven." She waited, but no one else emerged from the elevator.

"Not yet, Vytas," she warned. The first figure was still standing guard as the last of the others rounded the corner to the right, into the hallway. She had to ensure Vytas held his position until the guard left.

"Not yet."

The elevator doors started sliding toward each other, cutting through the glow lighting the foyer. The figure standing watch wasn't leaving.

"Not yet," she repeated.

Then, a black-gloved hand appeared from the light and gripped one of the doors, jolting the momentum to a stop before the doors began sliding open again. One last figure departed the elevator, illuminated by the elevator light.

"Eight," Alice concluded.

This one also had no weapon, but there was something else different. This one had removed the heavy cloak, choosing to continue on in much lighter apparel. She appeared to be female, wearing snug gray trousers, tucked inside heavy black boots and a dark jacket.

She stepped slowly past the one standing guard, moving in the same direction as the others. She was still wearing a helmet, and her face was hidden behind the tinted shield. The jacket was closed up to her neckline and tucked under the bottom edge of the helmet.

The guard turned to his left as the last one, presumably their leader, walked past, and then he followed her as they both stepped around the corner to the right, following the others.

"Vytas, you're all clear," Alice said, as she moved to the other monitor next to Kyle. "They are moving east down the hallway."

She muted her microphone and then pointed at the monitor, her finger touching the image of the figure second to last in the single-file line. "This one is in charge," she said to Kyle.

****

Vytas slid his body slowly toward the edge of the wall, just in time to catch a glimpse of the guard slipping around the corner. Then, he snuck quickly through the elevator foyer, barely noticing the weight of the axe in his right hand.

He stopped as he reached the north end of the foyer and pressed his body into the wall. He propped the axe against the wall and gently released the handle before peering around the corner. The guard was walking slowly behind the others, leaving about twenty paces of distance as they moved through the hallway.

Vytas knew the leader was approaching the third junction in the hall, so he had to make his move now. He loosened the sash that was wound around his left hand and ran up behind the guard as he snagged the other end of the sash with his right hand.

His long strides allowed Vytas to close the gap between them before the guard realized he was there. Vytas was at least six inches taller, so he easily slipped the sash over the guard's head and under his chin, just as they reached the hallway junction.

Vytas's wrists crossed in front of his body as he pulled up and back tightly on the sash, grimacing as he lifted the guard off his feet. He tilted his head to the side, out of the way of the guard's helmet, as he stepped backward during the struggle to the second junction to the main hallway.

The guard kicked Vytas's legs and clawed at his arms with his gloved hands; his weapon swung at his side, hanging from the strap draped over his shoulder. The animal skin cloak made the guard look heavier than he was, so Vytas was surprised at how easily he held his weight. He continued backward, turning right in the junction, out of sight, carrying the flailing guard with him.

The cotton fibers of the sash strained and dug into Vytas's skin as he squeezed the guard's neck tighter. The guard reached backward, still kicking and now swatting at Vytas's face.

He jerked from side to side, trying to avoid the guard's hands. He arched his back, lifting the guard higher off the floor. He felt the fight slipping away and then suddenly heard the voice in his ears: Liam's sweet voice.

[*"They need your help."*]

He had asked Liam earlier who needed his help, but he didn't know. The weight of the guard's body was growing heavier as he seemed to be giving in, then he stopped struggling all together. Vytas lowered the body to the floor and dragged it to the nearest door in the narrow hallway. He felt under the guard's helmet for a pulse.

He knew nothing about the intruders but was relieved to feel a slow, steady rhythm. The guard was unconscious but still alive. Vytas opened the door and pulled the body inside. He closed the door behind him, knelt next to the body, and freed the weapon caught beneath him.

Vytas hadn't thought much about what he would do when confronting the intruders. He assumed they were hostile. After all, they hadn't announced themselves, and they were armed. He guessed he would have killed them to protect the others, but then he remembered Liam's plea.

He looked around the small office, searching for something he could use. There were two monitors on the workstations with long, thin cables attached to the back. He ripped them free and returned to the guard, still passed out on the floor.

Vytas wound one of the cables several times around the guard's ankles. Then he slipped one end of the cable under the other and tied an overhand knot. He flipped the guard over on his stomach and brought his hands together behind his back before using the other cable to bind his wrists together.

He checked his work when he was finished, pulling on the cables. "You're not going anywhere, are you?" he said to the guard as he patted him on the back.

****

Alice and Kyle watched on one monitor as the intruders marched through the main hallway, while on another monitor, they could see Vytas moving in behind them.

Kyle examined the diagram on the monitor in front of him. "We can close off the hallway junctions toward the east end of the main hallway."

"We need to split them up," she suggested.

"If we force them to stay in the main hallway until they reach the east end," Kyle said, moving his finger through the hallway in the diagram as he plotted, "we can close this door after the first two walk through." He looked at Alice and waited for her approval.

"That could work." She nodded in agreement, looking at him over her glasses. "Do you need my help?"

"I got it." He spun back to face the screen and began tapping on the keyboard in front of him.

She turned back to the monitor in front of her in time to see Vytas duck around a corner, carrying the flailing body of the guard with him.

"One down, seven to go," she said to Kyle.

****

Vytas examined the weapon he lifted off the guard's lifeless body, trying to understand how to operate it. It was black with a short stock and a long barrel, similar to something he had been trained on in the military when he was young, but it seemed pretty basic.

"Alice," he said quietly. "Where are they now?"

"Still moving east through the main hallway," she reported. "Are you okay?"

"Yes," he responded, slipping the strap over his head and letting the weapon hang against his back.

"Kyle is closing off the junctions leading to the east end," Alice said. "We're going to try to split them up."

"That's a good plan." He stepped over the guard and made his way to the door at the opposite side of the room. "I'm working my way back into the main hallway. Make sure they stay in front of me."

"The group is still ahead of you," Alice said. "They haven't reached the blocked junctions yet."

Vytas reached the door and peered through the tall glass panel into the hallway before reaching for the handle, just to be sure. Then he gripped the doorknob and turned it slowly, pulling the door open just enough. Once he was sure, he exited the room and turned right toward the main hallway.

He stopped at the east end and poked his head around the corner. The others were far enough ahead that he was unable to see or hear them. He trusted that Alice had her eyes on them, so he quickly diverted west in the main hallway, backtracking to the elevator foyer.

He slowed down as he reached the left turn before coming to a complete stop. There, resting against the wall, just where he'd left it, was the axe. He picked it up and re-entered the main hallway; he began jogging east, closing the gap between himself and the others.

****

Alice's eyes bounced between several monitors as she tracked the intruders moving east through the main hallway and Vytas moving up behind them. She watched as he exited the office and emerged into the hallway junction and then toward the main hallway.

She turned quickly to catch of glimpse of Kyle in front of his monitor; she muted her speaker and asked, "What's your status, Kyle?"

He pushed a button on the keyboard in front of him. "I just closed the last of the hallway junctions; from L through the east end."

"Where's he going?" Alice wondered out loud, looking back at the monitor in front of her.

"Alice," Kyle called out, trying to get her attention.

She was distracted, watching as Vytas ran in the opposite direction in the main hallway. Instead of moving toward the others, he was heading for the elevator foyer.

"Alice, they're approaching L junction."

She jerked her eyes to the second monitor just in time to see the group leader stop in the main hallway as he noticed the closed security doors. The next five in the group gathered next to the one in front, while the last one, the one they believed to be in charge, halted behind them.

"They didn't expect this," Alice said to Kyle. As she glanced back at the other monitor, she noticed Vytas grabbing the axe he had left behind before jogging into the main hallway, heading east again.

The one in charge stood very still — waiting, watching — while the other five examined the situation. They were no doubt waiting for their superior to give the next order.

Alice clicked on her speaker. "Vytas, hold your position."

"What's happening?" he asked as he came to a stop.

"They've reached the sealed hallways," she reported. "They stopped moving at L junction."

Suddenly, the one in charge spun around 180 degrees, looking directly behind her. She screamed out an inaudible message after realizing the guard was missing. The others turned toward her, and they started running back, toward Vytas.

"Vytas, run the other way!"

****

He heard what sounded like shrieking coming from about a hundred yards in front of him. He winced at the sound, looking helplessly into the black emptiness for any sign of movement. Then he could hear the pounding footfalls coming toward him.

"Run back," Alice urged.

He quickly retreated back to the elevator corridor and ducked around the corner. He dropped the axe onto the floor and swung the pilfered weapon around in front of him. He gripped his right hand around the handle and his left hand around the barrel, pressing the stock into his shoulder. Aiming it straight up, he positioned his right index finger next to the trigger.

He could hear Alice mumbling in his ear, but he didn't respond to her. He just breathed deep and hoped that the weapon had no safety.

****

Alice watched wide-eyed as she observed her brother on the monitor. He appeared to be examining the weapon he lifted off the guard that he had disabled in the elevator corridor.

"Oh, my God … .what are you doing?" she wondered softly.

"Alice, just tell me when."

"They are closing in fast," she replied.

He closed his eyes and gripped the weapon tighter.

"Now!" she yelled.

He stepped around the corner and simultaneously lowered the weapon as he squeezed the trigger. The darkness retreated as flames spewed from the barrel of the weapon. He grimaced and squinted as his eyes adjusted to the bright glow. He could see that the two in front had been hit by the blast. They were screaming and swatting at the flames as they rolled on the floor.

The other five backed away from the flames as the two on the floor continued writhing around. Vytas's forehead was dotted with sweat beads from the intense heat that continued to flow from the weapon. As he swept left and right, he noticed the flames getting shorter.

He took a step backward.

The flame was sputtering now, and the other five began coming closer.

"Alice, I'm going to need some light." He slipped the weapon strap over his head and reached for the axe with his left hand as the last of the flames dripped from the barrel.

Three dark figures suddenly charged toward him. He flipped the weapon up and gripped the barrel in his right hand, holding it like a bat. He knelt down and swung the weapon at the one on his right, hitting him directly in the left knee with the butt of the weapon. The figure yelped in pain and landed in a heap on the floor.

Vytas then turned his attention to the one on his left. He didn't have time to ready the weapon for another swing, so instead, he kicked this one in the gut and then brought the weapon down on his back.

"Vytas, here come the lights," Alice warned.

He closed his eyes as the hallway was illuminated all at once by a burst of light. The other three screamed and clawed at their helmets as Vytas slowly opened his eyes.

"Night vision's a bitch," he said, smirking.

He dropped the flamethrower and gripped the axe in both hands as he leapt toward them. He brought the flat end of the axe down on the one in front and then flipped the axe around and swung the handle at the other one's head, meaning to disable them, not kill them.

One left, the one in charge. She was on her knees, gasping, still in pain from the sudden blast of light to her eyes. Vytas grasped her shoulder and lifted her to her feet.

He flung her hard, striking her head against the wall; she crumpled to the floor, unconscious. He knelt down beside her and slid the helmet off her head.

"Alice," he said, breathing hard, raising one eyebrow as he studied what had been hiding underneath the dark helmet. "You two better get down here. And bring zip ties."

Chapter 16

Alice and Kyle joined Vytas in the hallway and brought the zip ties from the security room. They also brought two rolling chairs to use as makeshift gurneys for the injured intruders.

"What the hell?" Kyle gulped as they approached the carnage left behind from the fierce battle.

Bodies were strewn about. The walls were scorched by fire, and there was blood staining the white floor tiles.

Vytas had removed the helmets from the two who were hit by the flamethrower's blast. They had gone into shock, unconscious, and were in need of medical treatment. Kyle quickly examined them from his wheelchair to confirm they were still alive, but he would need assistance to do anything further.

Vytas motioned for Alice to come over to him.

Two of the intruders who had charged at Vytas, the ones he struck with their own weapon, were now moaning and squirming on the floor.

"Quickly, quickly," he ordered as he grabbed one of them and flipped him over on his stomach. He held the man's wrists together while Alice fastened the zip ties.

"Now the other," he said, as he pounced over the one man and landed next to the other. He flipped him over and held his wrists while Alice secured him as well. He removed their helmets before making his way over to the one in charge. She was still lying motionless against the wall where Vytas had left her.

The one Vytas had struck with the flat end of the axe was still out cold, lying on his stomach. Alice grunted as she pulled his arms together behind his back and then fastened the zip tie around his wrists. She then moved to the one her brother struck in the head with the axe handle. He was lying facedown on the floor. She pulled his wrists together.

"Why do they all look … so odd?" Alice wondered out loud. She was still crouched next to the man, securing his wrists together while examining the eerie face of the one lying next to them. They were all hairless, no eyebrows, no eyelashes, nothing. Their skin tone was pinkish, almost translucent, and you could see their veins. She shook her head in disbelief.

They appeared humanoid but different, as if they had been living in total darkness. She removed the man's helmet once he was tightly secured and saw he looked the same as the others. She gently lifted his top lip, using the corner of her lab coat as a makeshift glove.

"No teeth," she announced, grimacing. "This looks like radiation poisoning, but they don't appear to be sick."

"Kyle," Vytas said; he had finished securing the zip ties around the wrists of the one they believed to be in charge. She was now awake and propped up against the wall.

"Kyle," he repeated loudly.

"Yeah," Kyle replied, flinching. "Yeah, I'm listening." He had been watching Alice as she probed at the man and couldn't help thinking that he had seen something like this before.

"How are the burn victims doing?" Vytas asked.

"Uh, they're alive," Kyle answered, turning his attention back to the other two intruders. "They need their burns treated, and they are still unconscious."

The one in charge was moaning. She began yelling incoherently and writhing violently against the wall, tugging hopelessly at the restraints behind her back and kicking her feet.

"That's enough," Alice yelled, smacking her hands against the floor.

The woman was panting, but for the moment, she calmed down. They were all staring at her.

"We need to get those two to the medical bay," Vytas ordered, pointing at the two burn victims. "We can secure these four in an office," he added, motioning to the ones he struck with their own weapon and the axe. "The offices lock, and we're the only ones who can open the doors."

Kyle turned his wheelchair as he started to sweat, and he could feel his cheeks burning. Vytas's voice grew further away as Kyle's thoughts strayed back years ago, before the Long Winter. He had done something terrible, and he couldn't help but wonder …

"What should we do with her?" Alice asked.

Alice's voice snapped Kyle back to reality. He knew he was going to have to answer for his past sins. He would have to tell them everything.

"I have some questions for her," Vytas responded, looking down at the woman. She was looking back at him with dead, lifeless eyes. It was impossible to tell by looking at her face what she was thinking or feeling.

"On your feet," Vytas ordered as he yanked her up by her arm. As soon as she had her balance, she wrenched her arm out of his grip. He gave her a shove. "Start walking."

"So," Alice teased, pointing at the foreign weapon still lying on the floor, "did you expect it to be a flamethrower?"

Vytas laughed, glad for the light-hearted moment. "Hell, no," he confessed. "But wasn't it cool?"

****

They led four of the prisoners into one of the small offices, sat them on the floor, and then zip-tied their ankles together. They made sure there was plenty of separation between them and then secured them with additional zip ties to table legs on the workstations.

As they closed the door on their way out, Vytas made sure it locked behind them. Then they made their way to the medical bay. It was the last room on the right side of the hallway, just before the lab, where Vytas had made entry with the axe. He and Alice were each pushing an office chair with the limp bodies of the burn victims. Kyle was leading the way, and the woman, the leader, was behind him.

****

Once their patients were stabilized in the medical bay, the next step was to return to the lab and question the woman. They had done all they could for the burn victims for now, but they would need more specialized care soon.

Alice opened the medical bay door while Kyle rolled through. Vytas followed, frog-marching the woman across the hall and into the lab. She wasn't struggling; there was no point. Whatever her plan had been, it had failed. Her entire group had been captured, including the guard who was meant to protect her.

The lab was brightly lit and quiet. Vytas slammed the woman into one of the chairs and rolled it against the far wall, where he could keep an eye on her. He pointed his finger at her and said firmly, "Stay." He walked over to Kyle and Alice and slid in between them.

The woman started screaming in her incoherent language, flailing in the rolling chair. She was angry and likely scared, thinking about what might happen next.

Alice whipped around and stared into the woman's empty eyes. She took a step toward her, and the woman stopped ranting.

Vytas pushed the hair from his sweaty brow and took a deep breath. He turned around toward them and exhaled heavily. "We need her to tell us why they are here," he growled, pointing at the woman.

Alice spun around, arms raised out to her sides, and stated the obvious: "We don't speak her language." She pushed up the wire-framed glasses on her nose as she added, "Besides, even if we could communicate with her, why would she ever tell us the truth?"

She had a point. Vytas leaned his head back, deep in thought. A memory was just out of reach. He turned his head away from Alice and Kyle, away from the woman, and stared at the floor, squeezing his eyes closed as he reached deeper in his mind. What was it?

Alice shrugged and said, "We can't even use a polygraph to question her."

Vytas suddenly lifted his head, eyes wide. He remembered something. "Yes, we can, Alice," he said, excitedly. "I need you to wake up my wife."

****

Alice and Vytas walked quickly to the chamber room. She scanned her badge and entered a six digit code on the keypad. The lock released with a loud clank, and they opened the outer doors.

"Are you going to tell me what your plan is?" she asked, as they stepped through the second set of doors and into the chamber. They stopped and looked dauntingly at the rows of silver pods that seemed to go on forever in all directions.

"Which way?" Vytas asked.

She pointed straight ahead. "That way."

"A polygraph measures blood pressure, pulse, respiration, and skin conductivity of a subject while they are asked a series of questions," Vytas began as they jogged past the rows of sleeping survivors. "You were correct that this wouldn't work on our friend. But there is another way."

She grabbed his arm to slow him down. "This way," she directed, pulling him to the right. She was panting as they jogged, out of shape and malnourished from the years she spent awake, waiting for the surface to thaw and the Long Winter to end.

"The best way to detect if someone is lying is to observe their body language and unconscious cues, in combination with pupil dilation and pulse," he continued.

"How do you know this?"

"Hanita educated me the night we met." He turned to face his sister as they continued jogging and winked as he smiled slyly, remembering that night.

She stopped in front of one of the pods. "Here," she said, trying to catch her breath. "She's in this one."

He walked up to the pod. It was hissing, and lights were blinking. Kyle had begun the waking process back at the lab. After a moment, there was a loud clang, and the pod door began to open. Vytas reached for Hanita.

"Wait." Alice gently grasped his arm. "Let her wake up first."

He obeyed his sister and waited, holding his breath. Looking at her now, it felt like yesterday when he watched her slip into the bio-suit, and he softly kissed the back of her neck. He remembered watching helplessly as she went into the chamber and began the Long Sleep. He pictured himself being back in the prep room, on the other side of the plate glass window, desperate to catch one last glimpse of her before she closed her eyes.

****

Hanita turned around in front of Vytas, and with her left hand, she gracefully pulled her hair over her shoulder, out of the way. He bent the top corner of the suit out of the way and paused to kiss the back of her neck. She giggled and shivered as his whiskers bit her skin.

He wrapped his arms around her body and leaned down, touching his left cheek to the right side of her face. She closed her eyes and folded her arms over his, feeling the cold fabric of the bio-suit he was wearing.

She opened her eyes and saw their reflection in the plate glass window in front of them. They were both outfitted in the black, iridescent fabric.

She closed her eyes and melted into his body, pushing the image far away.

[*Hisssssssss.*]

"What's that noise?" Hanita asked. She was no longer in Vytas's arms. Now she was facing him. He didn't seem to hear the noise and didn't answer her question.

"I will see you soon, my love," Vytas promised, stroking her shoulders. His deep-set eyes were warm comfort food: baked apples, speckled with cinnamon and dripping with caramel.

She moved her hands up his back. "Alice said this day will imprint on our minds," she whispered, looking up at Vytas with hope. "And we will dream about it."

["*Wait.*"]

"Who said that?" Hanita asked. It sounded like Alice, but she could see no one else in the room. It was just her and Vytas, but that didn't seem right.

"I cannot think of a better day to dream about."

Vytas's words caressed her and protected her like a velvet cloak. He swept the hair from her forehead with his fingers as he leaned down and kissed her lips. His embrace was her sanctuary; she retreated to it in times of stress and fear. She clung tightly to Vytas, confused and scared.

["*Let her wake up first.*"]

Hanita placed her hand on Vytas's chest, over his strong heart, and he reciprocated the gesture. As she slowly backed away, she suddenly realized she was already in the chamber, and Vytas was on the other side of the plate glass window.

Two men in white lab coats moved in around her. They started completing connections, making adjustments, mumbling to each other.

It was like she wasn't there. She was trying to speak to them, but they ignored her and kept doing their work.

"How did I get here?" she asked. She tried to get up but couldn't move. She could see Vytas and tried to reach for him, but her arm felt so heavy, she couldn't lift it.

The assistants finally moved away, their work finished, and there she was, alone. She tried screaming his name, but there was no sound. She was telling her body to get up, to walk out of the chamber and return to Vytas. But it was no use.

"This is just a dream," she started to tell herself. "This isn't real; it's just a dream." She closed her eyes and kept repeating it over and over as she heard the chamber hum and whir and hiss.

****

"What's happening?" Vytas asked Alice as he watched Hanita's eyes bounce back and forth under her closed eyelids. He took a step toward her and, again, felt Alice's hand on his arm.

"I think she's dreaming," she answered. "You were doing this right before you woke up."

Vytas recalled the images of the boy, Liam, and of Hanita. He *had* been dreaming of an actual moment in his life, but it had been altered.

"This is just a dream," Hanita began to whisper softly, over and over.

He wondered what Hanita was dreaming about. Would she also meet Liam? He was impatient and wanted her to open her eyes. He was holding his breath and struggling to keep himself from pulling her out of the chamber.

Just when he thought he couldn't wait any longer, her eyelids blinked open, and Vytas was able to breathe again. He went to her and cradled her cheeks in his trembling hands.

"V?" Her voice was raspy. She reached out to him.

Vytas took her hand in his and placed it on his cheek.

"V, is that you?" she whispered.

"I'm here, my love," he answered. "It's time to wake up."

****

There was no time for the reunion they had hoped for. Vytas and Alice hurried Hanita past the rows of silver cylinders, out of the chamber room, through the prep room, and back into the maze of hallways. It was so strange; where was everyone else? Hanita went with them because she trusted Vytas, but she couldn't help wondering why they were the only ones awake.

As they approached the doors to the lab, Vytas gripped the door handle and turned it. The handle clicked as he turned left and right, but the door would not open. He shoved his body against it, but something seemed to be blocking it.

"The door won't open," he announced, confused, looking at Alice and Hanita. He turned toward the door again and found the intercom.

"Open the door, Kyle." Vytas's voice blared through the intercom speaker, echoing through the lab and escaping to their side of the door.

There was only silence from the other side in response to Vytas's demand.

"What's going on?" Hanita whispered to Alice.

Alice was staring at the door, waiting for it to open. The only acknowledgment she was able to manage in response to Hanita's question was to shake her head.

As the speaker crackled from inside the lab, Hanita noticed the gray streaks in Alice's hair and wrinkles that had formed on her skin. And she knew the Long Winter had been more than five years. She turned away and watched as Vytas pressed the intercom button again.

"Kyle, open the door."

"Something's wrong," Alice said. She was still angry with Kyle, but that would not interfere with her feelings for him. He was a close friend and she cared about him; he just made some mistakes.

"Alice," Hanita whispered, placing a hand on her friend's shoulder. "Tell me what's happening."

"Kyle is in there with a hostile," she hissed, gritting her teeth together. "He could be in danger."

Hanita pulled her hand back and inhaled deeply. What had she woken up to? Had they made it all this way, only to encounter some other danger?

"I'm sorry," Alice said. "Look, I know you're confused —"

"We need to push the doors open," Vytas interrupted. "Maybe if we do it together?"

The three of them hurled their body weight against the door and pushed. They could feel it starting to give way, so they pushed harder. Whatever barricade was on the other side just needed a little more convincing to move out of the way. They continued shoving the door, until it was finally open enough to squeeze through.

Right away, they could see that Kyle had the woman against the left side wall of the lab, aiming the alien weapon at her. He must have snuck out into the hallway and retrieved it while Vytas and Alice went to the chamber room to get Hanita.

Vytas motioned for Hanita and Alice to stay behind him and slowly approached Kyle.

"How do you work this thing?" Kyle yelled.

He was shaking and sweating as he shook the weapon. It was obvious he had become frustrated by it. In his haste to complete his task before they returned from the chamber room, he had forgotten that Vytas had depleted the flamethrower.

"Kyle," Vytas said, breathing calmly, "let me have the weapon."

"No," he yelled. "You just want to stop me."

"That's not true. I want to help." He slowly stepped closer. "Will you let me help you?"

Kyle only groaned back as he continued pawing at the weapon. Out of his mind and feeling defeated, he lowered the weapon onto his lap. He began sobbing and started to roll his chair toward the woman, quietly waiting to be judged.

Kyle looked into her black eyes, his face streaked with tears and snot. "I'm sorry," he wailed, apologizing to her. "I'm sorry..."

Vytas quickly snatched the weapon out of Kyle's lap.

****

From across the room, Hanita studied the woman, still bound with zip ties and confined to the rolling desk chair in the lab. *Such a strange-looking creature*, she thought.

"Tell me again what you want me to do," Hanita said, turning to face her husband.

Vytas grasped her shoulders and looked deep into her eyes. "I know this is confusing, but I need you to trust me." His voice was soft but firm. "We may not have a lot of time, so I'm giving you the short version of events."

Hanita trusted him wholly. "Okay," she nodded, looking back at the woman.

He released her as she stepped away and began walking toward the captive. Her arms flowed naturally by her sides, shoulders relaxed, chin up. She purposefully projected confidence on her approach.

Hanita's eyes were fixed on the woman's. They were careful not to discuss their plan in front of her; they wanted her to be off-balance. Hanita stopped in front of her, and after a moment, the woman looked away, conceding the first battle.

Hanita seized her chin and pushed her head to the side, revealing the side of her neck. She could see a pulsing vein. Then she tilted the woman's head back so she could get a better look at her eyes. Her pupils were dilated. This could be normal, or it could be fear. Hanita leaned to one side, letting more overhead light illuminate the woman's face. Her pupils reacted quickly by contracting. When Hanita leaned back, blocking out the light, her pupils dilated again.

The woman grunted as she pulled away from Hanita's grip.

Hanita returned to Vytas' side and placed her hand on his arm to gently turn his body. With their backs now to their prisoner, she whispered, "I need to feel her wrist if I'm going to do this."

Alice stepped toward them. "Can you do it?" she asked.

"I can remove the zip ties and secure her to the arms of the chair," Vytas offered. "Will that work?"

"Yes, palms up, though." Hanita looked from Vytas to Alice and asked, "Who will be asking the questions?"

"I will," Vytas replied immediately.

"You're sure she can understand us?" Hanita clarified.

"Yes," he said. "I'm pretty sure she can." He had been watching the woman observe them, and he had a feeling that she understood them. She had reacted to certain things they said. She may not speak their language, but she certainly understood it. That's why he made sure they didn't discuss the plan in front of her. He didn't want her to know what was coming.

"Okay. Remember to start with a few control questions," Hanita instructed while Vytas nodded. "I'll let you know when I'm ready for you to move on."

Kyle sat quietly during this discussion. For everyone's safety, he had been restrained after Vytas pried away the weapon. They had not yet dealt with why Kyle had taken it upon himself to pass judgment on the woman. They had more important things to do first.

****

Hanita pulled up another chair and sat directly in front of her subject, their knees touching. She pressed her index and middle fingers onto the inside of the woman's wrist and wrapped her thumb underneath. "I'm ready," she said.

Vytas considered what control questions to begin with. It had to be questions they knew the answer to so that Hanita would be able to read the woman's nonverbal queues as yes or no responses.

"Is it true that you arrived in a group of eight?" Vytas asked.

This of course was true, so Hanita should be able to detect an affirmative response.

Hanita signaled to Vytas to ask the next question.

"Is it true that you are wearing gray trousers?"

Hanita nodded for him to move on.

"Is it true that the walls in this room are black?" This of course was false. The walls in the room were bright white in color.

"That was good," Hanita said. "Ask another negative response question."

"Is it true that you are from the Eastern Hemisphere?"

Hanita thought this was a good negative response control question. The Eastern Hemisphere had been destroyed by the explosion of Jupiter and rendered uninhabitable, so anyone living today was a Westerner, unless she was from somewhere else entirely. Hanita studied the woman's nonverbal response longer this time, not seeing the answer she was expecting.

Vytas was troubled by the long delay. "Nita," he said. "Should I move on?"

Hanita was quiet, still eying the woman and thinking. Then finally she looked at Vytas. "Ask another positive response control question," she said.

He looked back for help. "Helmets," Alice mouthed, pointing at her head.

He nodded and then asked, "Is it true you were wearing a black helmet?"

Hanita observed the woman's response, then without warning she took over the questioning and asked, "Is it true that you are from the Eastern Hemisphere?" Her eyes were locked on the woman's. "Something's not right," Hanita said.

The woman began screaming gibberish words at them and spitting as she grew angrier.

Hanita suddenly pulled her hand from her wrist and rolled backward slightly. Something the woman said …

"What's wrong?" Vytas asked.

Hanita listened as the woman continued to yell and thrash. Bits and pieces of what she was saying started to sound familiar, but why? Then, Hanita jumped to her feet.

"*Ustavi se*!" she yelled back at the woman.

****

"Remember that I told you that I traveled around with my parents when I was a child," she reminded Vytas.

"Yes, and you were homeschooled," he added.

"Right, well, I had a lot of teachers," she continued. "One of them spoke a language we don't hear anymore. One hundred-plus years ago, the planet was made up of diverse cultures." She looked back and forth between Alice and Vytas as she spoke. Kyle was parked away from their huddle, his wrists zip-tied together, starring at the other prisoner.

"After the Jupiter event, what remained of the population merged into something new," she continued, "and the old languages and cultures melted away. But some people remembered."

Hanita closed her eyes as she brought back the memories of her childhood. "There was this old woman in the east. She was my tutor-slash-nanny for many years while my parents were on assignment."

Hanita opened her eyes, smiling. "She spoke one of the old, long-forgotten languages … and she taught me in secret."

"You're talking about Saira," Vytas remembered.

"Yes," she responded, excitedly. Then she looked at the woman and pointed at her. "She is speaking that same language."

Vytas and Alice simultaneously turned their gazes toward their prisoner and then back to Hanita, still processing what she just said.

"They're not from here," Hanita added. "They are survivors from the Eastern Hemisphere."

"That's not possible," Vytas insisted. "There were no survivors there."

Alice slowly turned to face Kyle, her brow wrinkled with suspicion and doubt. Kyle's pitiful eyes were apologetic and wet. He noticed Alice glaring at him, so he quickly averted his eyes and refused to meet her gaze.

"I don't understand it, either," Hanita continued, "but it's the only thing that makes sense. We haven't been able to explore the red zone of the Eastern Hemisphere all this time, so we only assumed all life had been annihilated."

"But if they were there," Vytas wondered, "why didn't they contact us?"

Hanita shook her head, unable to answer his question.

Alice remembered Kyle's journal. He wrote about his failure to find rare earth metals in the amber zone after searching for months and how there would be no harm in exploring the red zone. *No harm*, Alice thought to herself.

"And you can understand her?" Vytas asked.

Hanita shrugged her shoulders as she studied the woman. "I don't know," she said. "Maybe."

"That's not exactly true," Alice interjected, slowly emerging from her trance.

"What do you mean?" Vytas asked.

Alice was still fixed on Kyle, watching as he squirmed in his wheelchair.

"Alice," Vytas insisted. "What do you mean? What isn't exactly true?"

Alice whipped her head around to rejoin the conversation with Vytas and Hanita. Her eyes bounced back and forth between them as the wheels turned in her mind. Then she turned back to Kyle in time to catch him looking at her before he quickly turned away again.

"Kyle has been to the red zone," she finally blurted out.

In unison, Vytas and Hanita both gasped loudly.

"Well, virtually," she clarified. "Kyle has been to the red zone virtually. Isn't that right, Kyle?"

Kyle did not respond and would not look at them. He was thinking about the journal that Alice had thrown at him, his journal. She had read his private thoughts. Why had he written about venturing into the forbidden red zone? His mind was racing as he tried to remember what else he had written about. What else did she know?

"You knew about that?" Vytas asked.

Alice stepped closer to Kyle and reached into the pocket on the side of his wheelchair. She pulled out the leather-bound journal he was trying to hide and waved it around like a prize in front of Hanita and Vytas. "It's all in here," she said.

Vytas snatched the journal from her hand and began to flip the pages. He could see by the handwriting that it was Kyle's.

"What is this?" Hanita asked, as she moved up next to Vytas to examine the evidence.

"Go on, Kyle," Alice prodded, "tell us about Dara."

Kyle felt his face ignite in a red glow. He was sweating, everywhere. The artery in his neck was throbbing noticeably as he searched desperately for the words, any words.

"Is she Dara?" Alice yelled, pointing at the woman.

"Dara is not a woman," Kyle said quickly, his voice cracking. "Dara is a place."

His eyes were wide, looking down at the floor, unable to meet their eyes. "I did go to the red zone, to Dara, but only to save us," he confessed. "We needed the rare metals to power us through the Long Winter." He paused, swallowing hard. His eyes were still wide, and he was shaking as he struggled to finish his terrible story.

"I know what I did was incredibly stupid," he admitted. "I went to Dara without approval," he said, pleading for forgiveness, "but that's all —"

"*Lažnivec*!" the woman screamed from across the room, sending a shock through their bodies. She kept repeating it over and over until finally, Hanita responded.

"*Tišina prosim*," Hanita said, raising her hand while she looked at the woman. "*Prosim*."

"What did she say?" Vytas asked.

Hanita turned away from their prisoner, now silent again, and looked directly at Kyle. "She says you're a liar, Kyle."

"And you believe her?" Kyle snapped, fuming. "She is not one of us."

"Kyle, you left an important part out of your story," Alice said.

He shrugged at her and grimaced, baffled by her comment. He still wasn't sure how much she knew about what he'd done. She said she had read the entire journal, but if she had, well, why would she be asking him to tell his story?

"I already told you all there is to know about the red zone," he stated. His eyes darted nervously from Alice to Vytas to Hanita and then back again. "I went into the red zone without authorization," he admitted. "That's where I found the rare metals used to manufacture the batteries that are keeping us all alive."

He began to breathe heavier. He wondered if he acted more confident in his story, if they would believe him. If he fought harder to make the woman out to be the enemy, would they accept what he was saying?

"If I had asked to mine in the red zone, you would have said no," Kyle directed to Vytas. "You should be thanking me."

"*Ne odpuščamo ti*!"

"What did she say?" Vytas asked Hanita.

Hanita thought for a moment. "I think she said, 'We do not forgive you.'" She looked at Kyle. "What does she mean by that, Kyle?"

He would not make eye contact with them; he looked away evasively and responded, "I don't know. You can't trust her."

"Do you think you can talk to her?" Vytas asked. "Find out what she knows?"

"It's worth a try," Hanita agreed.

****

Hanita slowly approached the woman and sat down in front of her. She gently placed her hand on the woman's restrained arm and smiled warmly at her. Vytas and Alice each pulled up chairs behind and on each side of Hanita. They stayed just far enough not to crowd and scare the woman but close enough to be involved in the conversation.

"What's your name?" Hanita asked, as she removed the zip tie from around the woman's right wrist.

"Marek," the woman responded.

"My name is Hanita." As she removed the zip tie from around Marek's left wrist, Hanita nodded her head to her left and added, "This is my husband, Vytas. And this beautiful woman on my right is his sister, Alice."

Vytas and Alice smiled at Marek, and she glanced uncertainly at each. She rubbed her wrists, both red and sore from the ligatures, and then she made eye contact again with Hanita.

"*Hvala vam,*" Marek said.

"You're welcome," Hanita responded.

"*Razumete moj jezik*?"

"Uh," Hanita said, looking at Vytas and then back at Marek as she considered her response. "I think I understand your language enough, yes. I'm hoping that you'll talk to me?"

Marek nodded and said, "Yes. *Govoril bom.*"

"Good," Hanita smiled. "Umm, can you tell us where you're from?"

Hanita listened as Marek told her story, stumbling along the way as she struggled to translate for Vytas and Alice. Marek said her homeland was called Dara. She referred to it as a special place in the Eastern Hemisphere that had collapsed into ruin but was once quite beautiful.

"So Kyle *was* telling the truth about that," Alice whispered to herself.

"What's that?" Vytas asked her.

"Nothing," she answered, glaring at Kyle. "Just something I'd been wondering."

"Marek, you do know that you're in the Western Hemisphere now, correct?"

"*Da,*" she responded. "Yes." She motioned excitedly toward the handheld navigation device she had stuffed in her satchel.

Hanita retrieved it and handed it to Marek. She was able to reverse their course back to where they originated from. Alice and Vytas watched as Marek showed them the coordinates on the device.

"It looks like they started here," Hanita said, pointing at the three-inch-square screen. She looked at Vytas and met his gaze. "That's two hundred miles inside the red zone."

"But that's impossible," Vytas doubted, looking directly at Marek.

"*Res je,*" Marek insisted, pointing at the screen on the handheld device.

"Marek," Vytas said softly, "the Eastern Hemisphere was destroyed when Jupiter exploded."

"*Ne, ne, ne,*" Marek responded, waving her hands. She leaned back in her chair and rubbed her forehead, thinking for a moment.

Hanita did not have to translate what was transpiring. It was obvious to Alice and Vytas; not wanting to rush Marek, they were giving her time to gather her thoughts before continuing.

"*Pred stoletjem,*" Marek began, "*nebo se je zakurilo in požgalo zemljo.*"

"She's describing the day Jupiter exploded," Hanita explained.

Marek relayed the events just as Vytas, Hanita, and Alice understood them from their own history books. She talked about the death and destruction that occurred; the mass graves of people who died from the original blast and subsequent radiation poisoning. How their satellite communications were also interrupted by the electromagnetic pulse.

"She says that they lost contact with the Western Hemisphere," Hanita said, looking at Vytas and Alice.

"Just like we lost contact with them," Vytas realized.

Marek took a breath as they absorbed what she had said, and she processed their responses. She listened as they spoke quietly to each other, not wanting to interrupt, but then she just couldn't hold it in any longer.

"*Smo mislili,*" she said slowly, "*zahodne poloble ni bilo več.*"

Hanita's mouth hung open as Marek spoke, just staring into her eyes.

"What did she say?" Alice pressed.

"She said," Hanita answered, "they thought the Western Hemisphere was gone."

"My God," Vytas breathed. "They were there all this time?"

Marek told of a day twenty years ago when a strange aircraft flew overhead. It made several passes over the entrance to their underground village before it hovered directly above them and landed. No one living had ever seen anything like it. So they only watched as the doors opened and a strange machine emerged.

"She's explaining Kyle's mining expedition," Alice realized.

"Twenty years ago?" Vytas questioned. "That means the Long Winter lasted —"

"Fourteen years," Alice finished, looking past Hanita to meet her brother's sorrowful gaze. "It was fourteen years."

"How did you … " He stopped before finishing his question. "I'm so sorry, Alice." He reached for her, and she placed her hand in his.

Alice wiped her cheek as a single tear made its way from her eye before smiling and turning her attention back to Marek.

"Prosim," Hanita said, motioning to Marek. "Please continue."

Marek explained that her people had learned how to survive underground. The machine began thoughtlessly drilling small holes in the ground where they lived and dropping its payload inside. After several minutes, the machine scurried back to the aircraft, drove inside and waited as the door closed behind it. They only watched from a distance, thinking it was going to fly away. But that's not what happened, not at all. Moments later, there were multiple explosions.

"Boom!" Marek shouted, mimicking an explosion with her hands.

One after another, the payload dropped into the holes drilled by the machine, erupted. There was screaming as their tunnels collapsed around them, trapping men, women, and children under huge piles of rubble. Those who were able ran deeper into the tunnels to escape the violence, but hundreds would be entombed.

As Marek told her story and Hanita translated, Kyle listened intently. He had known all along what happened that day. He watched safely from the lab as the tunnels were torn apart. He could hear the screams as he sent the mining robot back to collect the bounty.

Marek shook her head and sobbed, "*Bili smo nemočni, da bi karkoli naredili.*"

Hanita placed a comforting hand around Marek's. "She says they were helpless to do anything."

Alice reached for a box of tissue on a nearby workstation and handed it to Marek. "I'm so sorry," she said sympathetically.

"*Hvala vam,*" Marek responded. After a moment to dry her eyes and blow her nose, she was ready to continue her story.

She told how the machine emerged from the aircraft after the explosions and drove itself into the shaft it had created. They watched as it collected debris and loaded it into a bin it was towing behind itself. It made several trips before they decided to follow it, use their weapons to disable the machine and trap it. The aircraft eventually flew away without the machine.

Vytas looked back at Kyle, still listening to Marek's story. "You knew they were there twenty years ago," he repeated, "and you did nothing."

"*Umoril nas je*," Marek hissed.

"What did she say?" Vytas asked Hanita, still glaring at Kyle.

"She said, 'He murdered us.'"

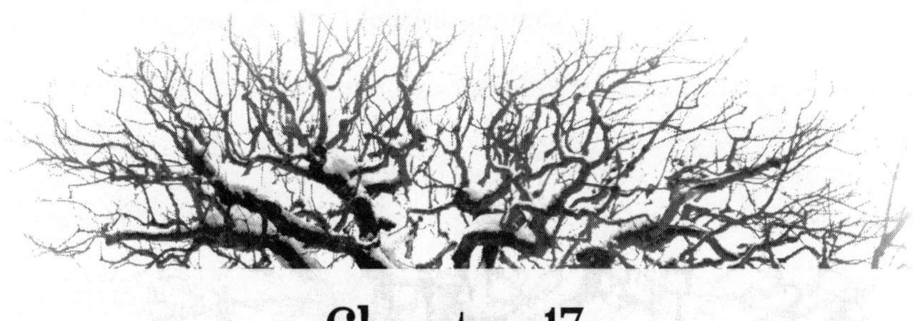

Chapter 17

Hanita's eyes fluttered open as dawn's rays tickled her long eyelashes. She was lying on her side, spooned tightly against Vytas's back, her arm around his waist. She squeezed him and snuggled into the crook of his neck, inhaling the scent of his skin. He moaned softly; he was still asleep.

Reluctantly, she rolled away and sat up, emerging from under the warm bedcovers. She swung her bare legs over the edge of the bed and gracefully slid her feet into the warm slippers placed neatly by the bedside. She paused there, gripping the mattress, holding herself up and staring at the floor. She was waking up.

She wrapped her arms around her body, suddenly feeling quite cold. One strap of her thin nightgown dropped off her shoulder. She glanced over at her robe hanging on the back of the bedroom door and then quickly stood up and scooted toward it, still rubbing her arms for warmth. She lifted the robe off the hook and slipped it on.

She gently pulled the bedroom door closed behind her and finished tying the sash of her robe as she made her way down the hallway. She glanced to her left at the closed door leading into the second bedroom and smiled before entering the hallway bathroom.

****

Vytas's eyes flickered open. He was lying on his back, in his own bed. He turned his head to find his wife, but her side of the bed was empty, covers pulled back. He turned his head back to the middle and closed his eyes as he inhaled the sweet perfume of pomegranates and cherries she left behind.

As he exhaled, jumbled images began rushing at him. He tried to grab hold of them before the images unraveled, but it was no use. He was waking up.

He sat up and swung his long legs over the edge of the bed, wincing at the feel of the cold tile on his bare feet. He rested his forearms on his thighs and stared at the floor.

He looked sideways and noticed the back of the bedroom door was bare. Hanita's robe wasn't there.

****

Before starting breakfast, Hanita made her way into the living room. Filtered rays of light were struggling to break through the window covering and claim victory over the darkness. She pushed the heavy drapes apart with a loud whoosh.

The boards covering the glass doors had been removed a year ago. The broken shards lying on the floor had been swept away, along with all the other debris remaining from the Long Winter. Now, everything was as it should be. She breathed in the beautiful sunrise. The horizon had turned fiery red as the sun cut into the purple sky.

Red and gold leaves peppered the streets and floor of the small balcony that overlooked city. Green grass was turning brown as the temperature dropped. Fall flowers were blooming. It was their first autumn since waking from the Long Sleep, and she marveled at the beauty all around her.

****

Vytas lifted fluidly off of the bed and then made his way to the washroom. As he relieved himself in the toilet, he tried again to remember the dream, but it was still just out of reach. He pushed the button, and the liquid swirled out of the metal bowl. He looked in the mirror, examining the fresh stubble covering his face as he washed his hands.

He turned off the water and dried his hands. As he reached the doorway, he expected to see Hanita standing across the room in front of the window, a memory from a long time ago. She wasn't there this morning, so he continued into the room and opened the bedroom door.

The hallway was dark except for the backlight from their bedroom and the light coming from the front room. The aroma of coffee and bacon filled the air. The door on the left was still closed, as was the bathroom door on the right. There was a slit of light peering from under the bathroom door, and he could hear water running. She was in there.

He paused in front of the door on the left, the second bedroom, before grasping the handle. He turned it slowly and then quietly pushed it open and stepped inside.

The walls were now painted a classic shade of blue; the former pale shade of gray, which resembled the most pastel shade of violet in the right light, was long gone. The dark wood flooring was now partially covered by a plush, cream-colored area rug. Sheer drapes with the leaf pattern in shades of gray that matched perfectly to the wall color had been replaced with heavy cream drapes.

The small desk and ergonomic chair were gone, replaced by a crib on the left side of the window and a changing table positioned on the right. The books had been replaced by stuffed animals and other child toys. The grown-up artwork had been replaced by diapers and baby wipes.

Cartoonish pictures of various animals decorated the walls now. A mobile hung over the crib had different shapes and colors of interest to a baby. Every detail of this room was perfect.

Vytas pushed the door almost all the way closed and then crossed the room to the crib. On the wall above it were four large, puffy letters: L – I – A – M.

Vytas placed his strong hands on the rail of the crib and gazed down on the baby, wearing a blue one-piece sleeper. Already awake, Liam's eyes diverted from the mobile above him to his father's face. He smiled and cooed, kicking his legs and bouncing his arms.

"How's my boy today?" He reached in with his right hand and rubbed Liam's chest. The baby reacted with toothless giggling at hearing the familiar voice.

"Oh, you're so heavy," he groaned as he lifted the baby with both hands from the crib. He held Liam in his outstretched arms for a moment, marveling at his beautiful son, his back to the bedroom door.

"You're Daddy's protector, aren't you?" he asked, gazing into Liam's caramel eyes. "You've always been Daddy's protector." Father and son shared a secret.

He pulled the baby to his chest and cradled him in his arms, rocking back and forth. It would be several years before he would hear the familiar voice again.

Looking over his left shoulder, he teased, "You're not fooling anyone."

"Am I that obvious?" Hanita asked from the doorway, surrendering to him.

"Perhaps we're just that good," he said playfully as he continued rocking Liam and turned to face her.

Hanita crossed the room to be with them. Vytas gently pulled his left arm out from under Liam and reached out for her, scooping her in close to his body. She put her right arm around his waist and with her left hand she stroked Liam's tiny forehead, pushing back wisps of blond hair and staring into his big eyes.

"He has your eyes, you know," she said, looking up at Vytas. "Just like his father's eyes." She raised herself up on her toes, and they shared a tender kiss. Her lips lingered on his before she lowered herself back to the floor. Then she turned and walked toward the doorway, singing back, "Breakfast will be ready soon."

Vytas, still studying Liam's face, reflexively replied, "We'll be right there."

He was thinking back to the day he awoke from the Long Sleep. He remembered the first time he looked upon the fair-haired boy with the sweet voice and caramel eyes who urged him to "Wake up."

Now holding his son in his arms, he asked, "Will you remember the day we first met?"

****

Hanita strolled down the hallway, past the kitchen on her right, and then rounded the corner. She stopped at the small table, set for breakfast. As she gently stroked the back of the highchair that had been added for Liam a few months ago, she thought about the cedar chest that once held baby clothes and blankets, passed down from her mother and hers before.

Before the Long Winter, Hanita couldn't bear to look at that chest, much less open it. The hope chest full of promises seemed empty and filled with lies. Until she found out she was pregnant, and then the first thing she wanted to do was open the hope chest with Vytas. And oh, what secrets it held.

She had sliced some fresh pineapple for their breakfast and arranged it on a plate, the first they had had since waking from the Long Sleep. Unable to wait, she plucked a slice from the plate between her first finger and thumb, and then glided across the living room to the glass doors.

As she gazed beyond the small balcony that overlooked the city, she took a bite of the pineapple slice. The sweet nectar landed on her tongue, and she moaned as she took it in. Juice trickled down her chin and landed on the floor as she took another bite.

She thought about the day she woke from the Long Sleep and met Marek. She recalled how she couldn't comprehend the story Marek told, that there was life in the Eastern Hemisphere after all, and yet they were still out of reach. The stories Saira had told Hanita about Dara when she was a little girl weren't just fairy tales; they were real.

Once everyone had been awakened, life slowly returned to normal. The previous Confederation, the one Vytas and Hanita had been part of, reconvened, and Vytas briefed them on what had happened the day Marek appeared. She was brave enough to address the Confederation herself, and Hanita translated for her. Her story about Dara and life in the Eastern Hemisphere was shocking.

A new summit would convene soon, but Hanita and Vytas would not be in attendance. They had served their time on the Confederation and had returned to private life. And they had a new purpose.

A purpose was hidden deep inside the hope chest. Wrapped in an unassuming scarf and tucked under musty receiving blankets and special baby clothes, Saira had left something very special for Hanita. She called it "the glory box." And in the sweet letter that accompanied it were very specific instructions.

This new Confederation, like the representatives before, would hear Marek's story. They would determine how to reach the survivors in the Eastern Hemisphere and reunite the world. Vytas and Hanita would go with Marek to Dara; they had to. They were determined to unravel the secrets of the glory box.

As Hanita finished the slice of pineapple, she noticed white flakes beginning to fall from the sky and settle on the piles of colorful leaves lying on the ground. Autumn was changing to winter right before her eyes, and she delighted at the sight.

To be continued ...